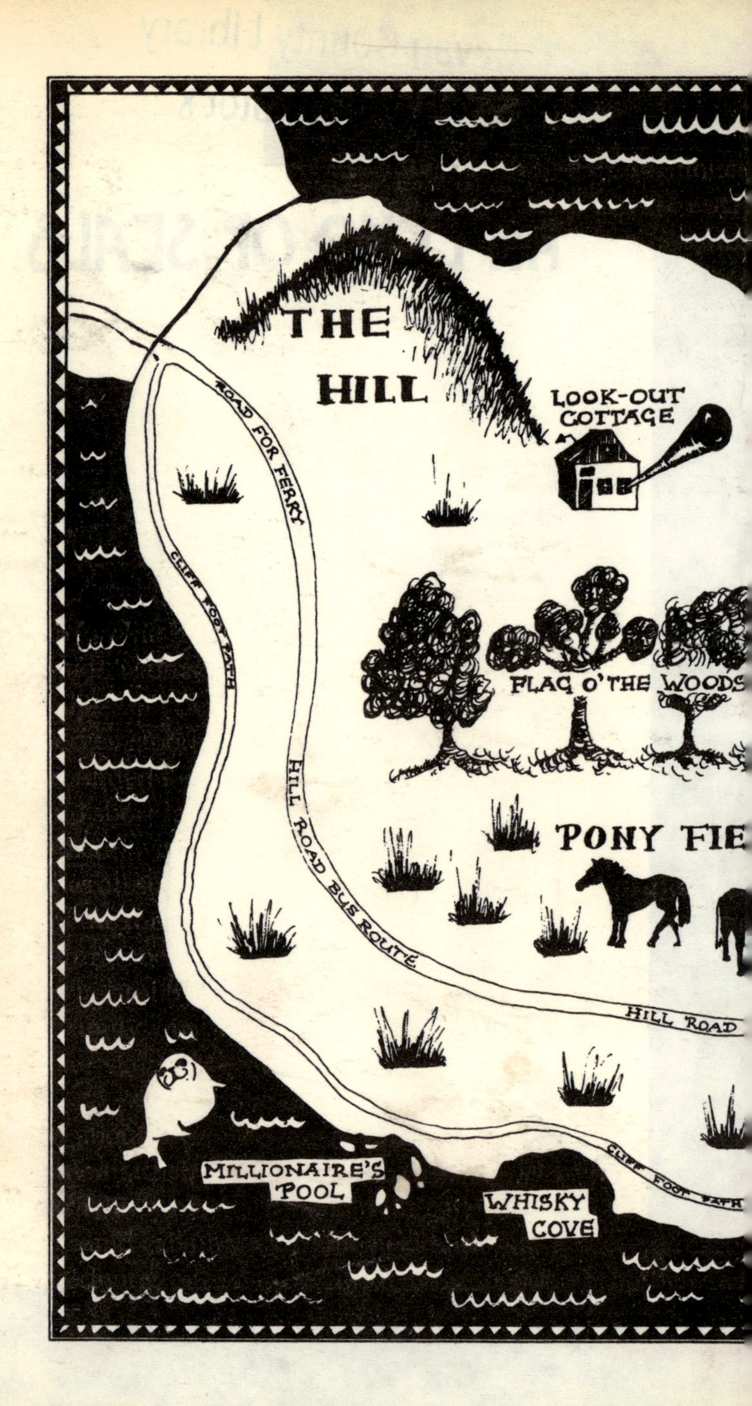

THE HILL
LOOK-OUT COTTAGE
ROAD FOR FERRY
CLIFF FOOT PATH
FLAG O'THE WOODS
PONY FIE
HILL ROAD BUS ROUTE
HILL ROAD
MILLIONAIRE'S POOL
WHISKY COVE
CLIFF FOOT PATH

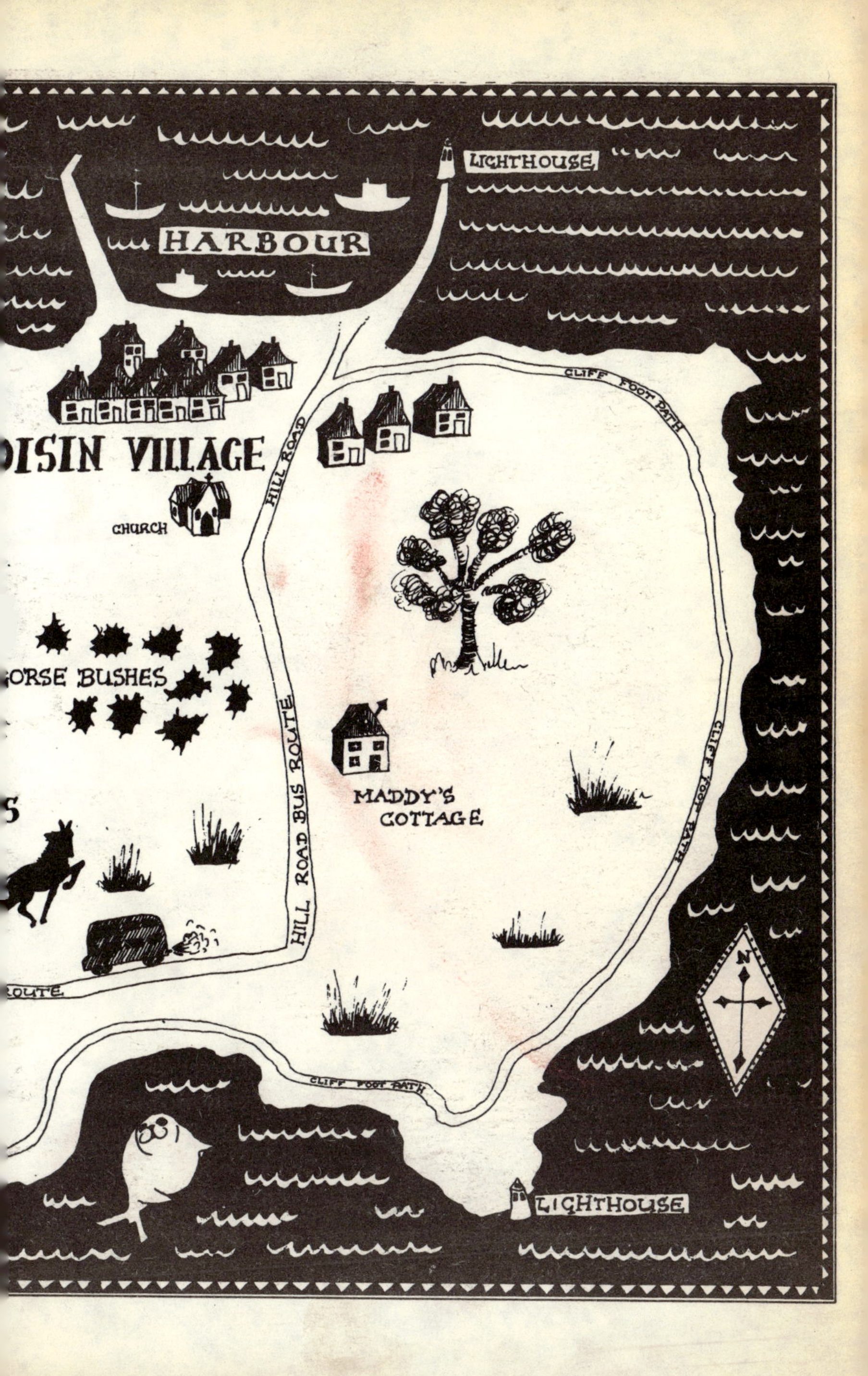
LIGHTHOUSE
HARBOUR
ISIN VILLAGE
CHURCH
HILL ROAD
CLIFF FOOT PATH
ORSE BUSHES
HILL ROAD BUS ROUTE
MADDY'S
COTTAGE
CLIFF FOOT PATH
OUTE
CLIFF FOOT PATH
N
LIGHTHOUSE

For Blaise and Gia

AN ECHO OF SEALS

ROMIE LAMBKIN

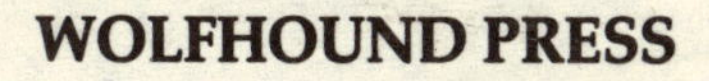

First published 1993 by
WOLFHOUND PRESS
68 Mountjoy Square
Dublin 1

Wolfhound Press receives financial assistance from the Arts Council / An Chomhairle Ealaíon, Dublin, Ireland.

British Library Cataloguing in Publication Data
Lambkin, Romie
Echo of Seals
I. Title II. White, Katharine
823.914 [J]

ISBN 0-86327-398-X

Typesetting: Wolfhound Press
Cover design and illustration, and text illustration: Katharine White
Printed by The Guernsey Press Co Ltd, Guernsey, Channel Isles

1

The Seventh Wave

Cold, cold, cold, tolled the chapel bell. On it went, and on.

The Hill of Oisín was silent except for the sombre bell announcing the children's funeral. It was not a proper funeral, though. There were no bodies to bury. The sea never returns the Oisín born, whispered the villagers.

Aideen and Ben stared out over the wide expanse of the still uneasy waters lidding the sea-bed.

'I don't like the funeral bell,' Aideen said.

Ben thought her eyes looked like glistening beach pebbles.

'I'm cold,' he said.

Cold, cold, cold, the chapel bell told the village lying in the cleft between the hills, as it had done other mornings after a storm, a shipwreck or a cliff-fall or, as now, the drowning end to a game of Dare played with the waves of the sea. Ben supposed he must have heard that gloomy booming before because he remembered seeing dark crowds crawl uphill to the church which split the road into two, one that outlined the coast, the other going inland, up the pane-of-glass hills to West Mountain where the television bouncer mast stood keening to the wind. But those past funeral bells had wafted by him like air as he free-wheeled his bike downhill to Aideen's. He thought now of the funeral service held for Tom Sawyer and Huckleberry Finn.

'Everyone thought they were drowned, d'ye remember?' he reminded Aideen, 'and when they walked into the church everybody nearly fainted.' A gleam of wintry hope lit his face.

'Fintan and Declan won't come back.' Aideen's voice was clear, cold, 'Oisín born and all that.'

'But if it was one of us?'

'We'd be washed up on Movare Beach on the next tide, or on Marock Strand the day after.'

'We'd be dead,' said Ben.

'Like Declan and Fintan.' She flashed him another pebbly glance.

'But I still can't believe they're dead. No one's seen their bodies. I mean where *are* they? Even if they were born in Oisín, they must be *somewhere*. Oisín people must have been drowned around here for hundreds of years. Where *are* they all?' His disbelief in the legend was passionately clear.

'You don't come from here, that's why you can't believe it,' she said.

'Neither do you. Not properly.'

'No, but I *am* Irish and we've lived here since I was small.'

'I'm as Irish as you are!' Ben was indignant.

'Yes, but you've always lived in England, except for the summer holidays, that's the difference.'

~

Only Aideen knew the depths of Ben's longing for Oisín all the other months of the year. He has two faces, she thought often, one of wide smiles all summer long, the other darker one, broody, when he and Aunt Riona waved goodbye from the deck of the ferry, Liverpool bound. Aunt Riona had the same two faces, as a matter of fact, though it did not show so much since she started college. Aideen frequently envied them the sea voyage and the long drive eastwards on England's motorways in their red Mini.

'I wish I was coming with you, Ben,' she would say.

'No, you don't,' he always answered. 'You wouldn't like it at home. It's nothing like here, you know.'

She did know. He had told her. His was a house of cold silence or hot quarrel when both his parents were in it, so it was better that his father spent little time there. 'He's always in the pub,' Ben explained, 'and he's not very nice when he's been at the pub for a long time.' Ben never noticed his heavy sigh when he said things like that, but Aideen did. He did not ask school friends home much for that reason. During the dark winter months he constructed Airfix planes, played records, did homework, watched TV or played chess and cards with Aunt Riona.

'Mum's great really,' he would say, 'she takes me and Barney and Sooty out fishing and swimming, things like that.'

Barney was his best friend, and Sooty was his black,

tan and white half-Collie, nearly four feet tall when he stood on his back legs. He had a face like a happy lion. Ben always carried a photograph of Sooty.

'I do love Dad but ...' he would end, the sentence stuck in his throat, incomplete.

Although they never said so, Ben and Aideen loved one another like the brother and sister neither had. 'What you never had, you never miss!' Ben quoted Aideen's mother whenever the subject of only children arose. 'Absolutely right,' Ben's Aunt Maddy would join in, laughing. Her black hair top-knot made her even more ballerina-ish, he thought, and that was lucky as she had to teach ballet twice as much since Aideen's father died a few years back. The children wrote to each other regularly between the summers. Aideen would tell Ben what the summertime gang was doing — never as exciting as in the hot days of July and August when they had all gathered together at Flag o' the Woods, in the field below Far Hills cottage. 'Declan and Fintan are always in trouble for trespassing,' she wrote, and 'mitching' from school, stealing apples, or riding other children's ponies (as they had none of their own), and so on, and so on. Ben would smile as he read Aideen's letter, remembering Declan and Fintan, the Terrible Twins, as they were known locally, although they were not twins at all, not even brothers; and he would remember how all of them, himself, Aideen and Ferna, Brains, Micky, Nuala (and Mac Alúishin, although you never could be *sure* what Mac Alúishin was doing) followed those Twins on out-of-bounds cliff climbs and scrambles across ragged rocks overhanging deep waters. Declan and Fintan always chose the highest trees to climb, daring Ben to follow. 'Come on, ye're afraid, ye English coward', they would jeer at him, laughing, white teeth gleaming in their tanned faces.

'I'm not English and I'm not a coward either,' he would shout back when he reached the quivering top branch of their challenge. He would be quivering inside too but that he hid from them.

'Yerra, ye're a grand man,' Declan or Fintan would say, and begin the jumping-down-from-the-tree game.

'I'll tell on you!' Aideen would shout at the three of them, watching them drop twelve, fifteen, twenty feet. 'It's a wonder you're not dead!' As she sometimes shared in the tree jumping game she did not tell.

The days of Gale Force winds 9 and 10 entranced them. As it was too rough to swim, they dodged the waves thrown across the Beach Road by angry seas, shrieking themselves to a fever pitch, getting drenched, not caring. The most exciting of the storm waves reared up and over the top walk-way of Oisín's East Pier in huge sprays and waterfalls of white foam and glittering aquamarine sea waters.

'Danger! It is dangerous to walk near the sea slope after sunset or in stormy weather.'

The large red notice beside the Pier's stubby entrance pillars said that, so there was no excuse.

'It was all my fault.' Ben's sudden shout of grief jerked Aideen from her own rememberings.

'No it wasn't. It wasn't. *It wasn't.*' Aideen's voice shrilled higher at each repetition. Then it sank to a whisper. Ben strained to hear. 'It was *their* fault. They shouldn't have dared you.'

She said what both of them had been afraid to say for

three days. Ben felt as if he had come out of prison. She was right. The Terrible Twins *had* dared him to race along the Pier's top level and down the first set of steps in order to beat the seventh wave. They always counted the waves and the seventh was the biggest. When he reached half-way, Fintan and Declan knew Ben would not make it. They had forgotten his knee still lacked strength after the cartilage operation. As one, the Twins hurled Aideen backwards and threw themselves after Ben in wild despair. Their frantic arms pushed him over the edge to the lower, harbourside level where Ben had grasped an anchorage post as the last of the seventh wave washed over him. He saw Aideen screaming in terror, her black hair strealing like seaweed in the wind.

'They're *gone* ... I can't see them ... *they're gone*!' she cried, aghast.

The gigantic wave had fallen back, ready for the next assault, raking and rolling Declan and Fintan down the seaward slope of granite rock like fallen leaves.

The coastguards came running. The lifeboat was launched. No lives were saved.

2

Kerumph, Kerumph!

'It'll be over now.' Ben pressed the time button on the digital watch he had bought from the ferry's duty-free shop. He waved it under Aideen's nose, making her take her fingers from her ears.

'Twelve o'clock, is it?' Plugging her ears had blocked the bells. 'It feels like the whole day has gone. Our Mums will be home by now, probably.'

Maddy and Riona had gone along to pay their respects at the Church, as the custom was, but they understood when Aideen and Ben said they wanted to remember Declan and Fintan up on the Hill by themselves.

'But we needn't go home yet,' Aideen said, 'it'll be a late lunch and I want to run and run and *run*. What about your bockety knee?'

'Never mind that. You run as fast as you like. You can wait somewhere for me to catch up,' said Ben.

'Where will I wait?'

He hesitated. 'The harbour?'

'*The harbour*?' Her voice sounded thin.

'Not the East Pier end ... the other side. We could watch the reconstruction work for a bit.' Even as he spoke, the warning siren gave one of its deafening daily blasts: two minutes to go for the next dynamiting of the harbour floor.

'Let's go,' Aideen shouted. She jumped down to the narrow cliff path and ran along it to Scadeen Bay, downhill, downhill, at full speed until she blew herself out into a jog trot beside the sea-front wall and the bowling green grass alongside it. She dropped full length on the smooth grass to slow her heart beats and wait for Ben. He was a bare half minute behind her. He is running faster, she thought.

Kerumph! Kerumph!

The water heaved itself into an uneven waterspout. Once. Twice. Once more.

'You'd think that with all that sirening, and "*Danger*" notices everywhere, that it'd be more than that, wouldn't you?' Aideen sounded impatient. 'Every time I see it happen I think I won't bother to watch again, but I always do.'

Ben stood on the wall near the '*Keep Out! No Entry! Danger! Reconstruction Work*' noticeboards. 'But just look at how much they've done, Aideen,' he said. It reminded him of those pictures in encyclopedias, showing vast reservoir barrier walls where workers and machines toiled like ants miles below. 'They look like Action Men playing with Matchbox trucks and excavators down there. It's *huge*.'

There had been a great public outcry when Oisín harbour alteration plans first became known. Everyone protested. They will ruin the harbour, they said. Why can't they leave it alone? It's just right as it is. All the local shops put petitions on their counters for people to sign. Objection meetings and marches were held, committees were formed, but the local government councils explained that the harbour was silting up so fast that, soon, the water would be too shallow for the fishing smacks to anchor. They said the reconstruction would include a dry dock for fishing boat repairs, a yachting marina and gardens to border the whole sea front. The new harbour, they said, would make Oisín more attractive than ever.

Aunt Maddy just snorted. 'That's what *they* say,' she said.

'It's hard to believe all right.' Ben surveyed the all-embracing mass and mess of liquidy, chocolate-coloured goo before their eyes. 'Everything everywhere is just mad. Look at them scooping up more and more mud from the bottom this very minute. I suppose the cranes and things are that bright yellow colour to make them easy to see. I'd rather fancy one of the men's yellow protective helmets, mind you!'

'It was worse when they started,' said Aideen. 'You should have seen them trying to keep the sea out. I wrote to you, remember? As soon as they'd built up that big new jetty, to join the wall outside the Yachting Centre on the West Pier to the wall over there, the sea would sneak round it. And those ee-norm-ous lorries loaded with rocks the size of cart horses would get stuck in the mud and the caterpillar tractors had to drag them out before the next high tide.'

'You see those huge, bendy sort of hose pipes?' said

Ben, 'I've been thinking — they keep the harbour bottom dry the same way as that sucker thing the dentist puts in your mouth when he's fiddling at your teeth. It's pretty terrific really. I mean, look at those girders. They must be forty or fifty feet long. Look, there, where only the girder tops are sticking out of all that great concrete wall. I mean, how *many* of those massive girders did they use?' His brain was whirling. 'D'you think they're inside all the walls of the original piers too? It's fabulous really. I wonder how long the whole thing will take.'

'Well, it's been nearly a year and it's supposed to take two, but Mum says it'll be more than that. They're going very deep.'

'Too deep, I'd say,' said Ben.

'People in the village have been saying that for ages, mostly the older ones. They say the sea bed shouldn't be disturbed. Even Mum thinks that a bit.' Aideen laughed. 'She says there's a grain of sense behind most superstitions.'

'Like about the Oisín born?' Ben blurted. He babbled on, anxious to fill the emptiness lurking within them. 'What about that revolting sea front mud-mountain they've manufactured from the sea bed mud? You can't even see the island any more with that plonked in front of us like that. Or are they going to throw it all back in when they've cemented everything, or what? Your Mum's right, it is an eyesore. It makes my eyes sore to look at it this minute.'

'Mine too!' The comment came from a man riding past them on his cream-coloured horse. He must have heard Ben's tirade. Something about the man and his foamy-tailed horse stirred Aideen's mind.

'In a way, I'd like to go down there,' Ben carried on, so intent he heard nothing of the interruption, 'there must be fossils, and the old bottles ..., they're valuable now, you know, and coins ... all sorts in that mud.'

'Fishermen's false teeth and pirates' treasure too, I suppose.' Aideen's sense of humour was shadowing about, getting ready for a comeback.

'I bet those men down there find things just the same,' Ben muttered. 'Probably make a packet selling them too. Maybe, if I had a metal detector ....'

'Do they have those in the ferry's duty-free shop as well?' she jeered at him. He looks excited, she thought, pleased.

A loud pounding of hooves on the turf of the bowling green made them turn. The horse and its rider galloped by at full speed, back the way they had come. 'Oh.' Aideen was furious. 'There'll be chunks out of the turf and hoofmarks everywhere. The gardener will go berserk.' But not a mark showed on the green sward.

'The ground must be very hard,' said Ben. 'Will you look at the speed of them — I didn't even see them turn the corner to the hill, did you? You'd think they'd galloped straight into the sea.'

'Anyway,' said Aideen, 'horse riding up there on the cliff is forbidden, you know that, so it's good enough for them to gallop into the sea. I hope they drow ...' Appalled at herself, she stopped. 'I didn't mean ...'

'I know you didn't, it's just the way we always joked — before — before —' Ben stopped, then he added. 'Something about that man is niggling around in my head. Who is he, d'you know?'

'No. I was wondering myself but ... no ... anyway I'm

hungry all of a sudden, and there's the Hill Bus over at the station. Let's run for it.' She ran, reaching the bus stop just in time.

He jumped on the bus behind her. 'Got any money?'

'No, but it's Mr Carrigan driving, didn't you see? He'll let us pay him on the way back.'

Everyone on the Hill knew Mr Carrigan since the days of the tram, which was what he drove before the Hill Bus took over. Now bramble bushes grew over the tram tracks and the Hill Bus had a new roadway. Mr Carrigan told the children stories of the days of the tram as they rode his bus back and forth to school, or in their holidays. He knew every local passenger by name and their friends and relatives when they came to visit. People used to run to a tram stop and ask Mr Carrigan to buy them a pint of milk, a loaf of bread or a newspaper from Connolly's shop down at the cross, which he duly delivered to them on the return journey. Aideen and Ben could remember that sort of thing happening when they first used the Hill Bus, but not now.

'Everyone goes to the supermarket in their cars these times.' Mr Carrigan was wistful. 'Sure them were the days.' He gave them his usual crooked-toothed smile when they said they would pay their fares on his return run. 'Grand,' he said. 'It's a bad day for you, isn't it? I'll miss them myself. We all knew when the Terrible Twins were on the bus, didn't we? Ah, sure, they're in a better place, God bless them.'

The bus growled up the steep incline in low gear until it reached the Summit where the whole bay opened out before them and, directly opposite, the land curved out the ups-and-downs of the Wicklow and Dublin mountains, the Sugarloaf's point above them all. The name had puzzled Ben when he was younger. Its shape was not like a loaf as he knew it, thinking of bread, but when he thought of the conical shape sugar made when it was poured into a pile from the packet he was satisfied. Local people called the mountains the Far Hills, the name written on the tree outside Aideen's cottage because its windows looked directly at them. Even when the sea was grey and the mountain tops coming and going in cloudy mist like today, Ben's chest lurched upwards as he looked their way. On a sunny day though, when the sun shone gold and the sea stretched itself into a sparkling carpet below them, the Far Hills' outlines sharpened and seemed close enough to touch. That made him take off inside like a bird. He liked the feeling.

Mr Carrigan stopped the bus at the cottage gate for them.

'I suppose you'll be off down to Flag o' the Woods after your dinner, ' he said. 'That's the right place for all of you today, isn't it? You were all friends there, weren't you? Mac Alúishin and all.' He drove off, leaving a wraith of exhaust in the air.

Aideen and Ben stood like statues.

'How did he know about Flag o' the Woods?' Ben asked.

'Mac Alúishin,' said Aideen softly. 'I'd forgotten about Mac Alúishin.'

3

Mac Alúishin

Mr Carrigan was right. They were all there ... well ... no one knew for sure if Mac Alúishin was there yet. Declan and Fintan had always known that first. There he is! one or the other would say, glancing to the opposite corner of the field where the thicket of blackthorns huddled around a lightning-struck tree on the Island. The Island was a small mound circled by boggy pools, where the stream flowing from Flag o' the Woods seeped into the ground. Mac Alúishin's presence would fizzle into all of them like an injection of Esso Extra some seconds afterwards. Who would be the first to know now?

'He's there,' Aideen whispered, and knew she was the one.

They looked towards the Island, the familiar fizzing waking in their veins.

'I don't know why we always look,' said Ben. 'We never see him, do we?'

'I can't help looking,' Aideen admitted.

Nuala's long eyelids slowly blinked over her violet

coloured eyes. 'I know it sounds stupid but I always feel he's beckoning to me even though I can't see him.'

'I just like knowing he's there.' That was Brains (really Brian), an eight-year-old whose intelligence and general knowledge constantly confounded the others, his elders by three or four years.

As usual, thought Ben, he's right on the button. It's just as well we like the little divil. But just knowing was not enough for today.

'I wonder ....' Ferna used a churchy whisper instead of her normal shrill chirrups. She stopped.

'What?' asked Aideen.

'Well, I wonder ....'

'Oh, go *on*.' Micky had no patience with his sister. ('A saint would get impatient if he had six sisters in a trail behind him like me,' he would excuse himself from time to time.)

'Well ... do you think Mac Alúishin knows?' went on Ferna at last. 'I mean, do you think we ought to tell him?'

It was a new angle. Micky no longer appeared quite so hasty, rather as if here was something more concrete for him to grab, a thing to *do*, to fill up the empty space in the middle of them where Declan and Fintan were not. Like Black Holes in space, he thought to himself, his sharp face burning red along the cheekbones. He stood up.

'It'd be no harm trying,' he said, 'even if he doesn't *want* us to see him.'

'Or we're not able to, you mean,' Ferna interrupted. 'I mean, after all, not one of us ever has.'

'OK ... OK' said Micky. 'Whether he doesn't want us to, *or* we're not able to — whichever it is — it's only fair to tell him ... although I bet he does know.'

Ben did not remember them talking about Mac Alúishin like this before. He tunnelled about in his head to pinpoint the first time he knew about Mac Alúishin but without success; he just must have absorbed the knowing, the way blotting paper absorbs ink. I suppose that's how it happened with us all except, maybe, the Terrible Twins. I wonder if the Oisín born bit made any difference about Mac Alúishin.

'Are you coming or not, Ben?' Aideen stood over him, prodding his ribs with the toe of her flip-flop.

Micky led the way, striding out fast until the outer branches of the Island blackthorns almost tipped his chest. There he stopped, as if a stone wall hindered him.

'Go on. Jump on to the Island,' urged Ben, 'we're right behind you.'

'I — I — I can't.'

A scraping, rustling sound came from the massive nest of tangled ivy which sat like a gigantic mob cap on the top of the dead oak tree. They backstepped from the boggy pools, narrowing their eyes against the sunlight, trying to penetrate the leafy thicknesses.

'Mac Alúishin,' called Ferna, 'we want to tell you something, and it's not very nice either.'

'Oh, shut up, Ferna, that's not Mac Alúishin,' said Micky. 'He's not going to go climbing trees. If he's anywhere, he'll be in the blackthorn bushes.'

Ferna stood her ground. 'How do you know, Micky O'Mara? You don't know what he does any more than we do.' Her indignant glare swept the others. 'He doesn't, does he?'

'No,' Aideen said. 'None of us know what Mac

Alúishin does, or where he goes when he's not here.'

'I'm going to tell him, then.' When it came to decision-making, Ferna's speed always took them by surprise. She shaped her hands into a loudhailer. 'Mac Alúishin! We want to tell you, just in case you don't watch television or read newspapers or anything like that, well ... you know our friends, Declan and Fintan? Well, they're drowned. They're dead. You won't see them any more. That's what we want to tell you.'

'Yes. And we're lonely without them!' Aideen shouted, although she had not meant to.

Micky threw his thought at the tree like an angry stone. 'We miss them something rotten.'

An eerie cry sounded. The dead oak tree's untidy ivy crown rattled and crackled as if in the teeth of a gale, but no gale blew. A thrust of air ejected a heavy body skywards, its great wings flapping languidly, powerfully, its long black neck and small head stretching forward, uncontrolled, twiggy legs trailing behind the chunky body. It hovered a moment over the silenced children, then soared over the headland, beyond the field they stood in, and dropped down towards the sea, out of their sight.

'What kind of a bird is *that*?' Ben looked at Brains. Would he know?

Brains shook his head. 'Too big for Ireland.'

'Have you ever seen a bird like that round here?' Aideen asked Micky.

'I have not,' he replied, 'nor at home in the country either.'

'Well, there's one thing,' Nuala said, her eyelids rising and falling in slow dramatic sweeps.

What? Ben wondered. Don't tell me *she* knows.

'My Mac Alúishin feeling has gone.' Nuala looked at their dismayed faces. 'So has yours. I can see.'

'You mean,' said Aideen, 'that *he's* gone, as well as that peculiar bird? Maybe it has escaped from Dublin zoo. Storks and flamingos do sometimes.'

'No. I don't mean that,' said Nuala. 'I mean that it might be Mac Alúishin.'

'*A bird*?' Ben rocked in shock. Nuala must be going funny.

The others laughed uneasily, thoroughly taken aback.

'Well, why not?' Ferna sprang up, her eyes challenging them. 'As Ben said, we've never seen him. We've never even talked about him before, not really. We just liked the feeling he was there, at least I did. Maybe, now, we should try to think *what* we thought ....' Her tongue tripped with excitement. 'What do *you* think he is, for instance, Micky O'Mara? How do you see him inside your head? You've always got a lot to say about everything.' Although Micky was her brother, she always called him by his full name for no reason anyone knew, including herself.

'We should *all* say,' Micky said. 'You begin, Ferna, you're the one to begin.'

Ferna said nothing.

'See,' said Micky, 'she's stuck. She doesn't know what's inside her head.'

'Leave her alone,' said Aideen. 'I don't know what I think myself, not absolutely, but something's coming, if you'd just be quiet a minute.'

'It's like turning the TV knob for a better picture when

it's all fuzzy.' Ferna spoke slowly. 'It's still fuzzy, but Mac Alúishin's green, his clothes are I mean. Or her clothes are. There's a skirty bit. It could be a smock or a tunic. She — yes, I'm certain sure she's a she — she has a lot of goldish hair and a floaty little cloak with an enormous brooch on it with all sorts of patterns, and she's about the same size as me, and,' she seemed surprised, 'she's a part of me too.' She sank down on the warm grass and lay flat. 'I'm tired.'

Aideen crouched down beside Ferna, bent knees shining a deep tan which shaded into a paler, coppery gold as the upper leg sloped towards her scarlet shorts. She seemed to be puzzled.

'No. Mac Alúishin is a little *man*,' she said. 'I don't mean a dwarf and I don't mean anything silly like a leprechaun, just an ordinary *man*, but small, about your height, Ferna. You're right about that, and he does wear green, a kind of ski suit and a woolly ski cap with a bobble. He's kind and laughing, and he loves children. That's why he comes to the Island when we're playing, and that's why he follows us whatever else we do in the day. But he goes home at night.' She paused, then added, 'He's probably some sort of tramp, a bit simple in the head, in a nice sort of way. But his love is very strong. I always feel it warm all over me.'

Micky had listened very attentively but now he burst out. 'The only thing you're both right about is that Mac Alúishin sort of, well, *wants* each one of us, or' (his hard-headedness found it hard to say this) 'he loves us like you said, Aideen. But,' he went on, 'neither of you said anything about that huge bird, the albatross or whatever it was.' He used the strangest sounding bird name he knew. 'Even Nuala said it could be Mac Alúishin. Well, maybe it could because I think Mac Alúishin has great powers ....'

'Powers?' Ben felt an odd squirm in his stomach.

'You mean supernatural powers? Mm, there's a lot of that about in some parts of Ireland,' Brains said, sounding like a doctor dealing with an outbreak of chicken-pox.

'Kind of,' replied Micky. He was still unwilling to leave his commonsense world. 'But *something* stopped me getting on to the Island. It felt like bumping into an invisible inflatable dinghy. That greeny colour he wears is sea-green, and the tunic thing goes into jaggy layers like waves, with creamy edges even, and he often gleams all over as though he was wet, and he wears small frogman flippers, only they're green, not black like mine. He has a little cloak, like you said, Ferna, only it's as if it was made out of that thin, bright green seaweed Nuala calls Mermaid's Hair. I think he has a lot to do with the sea.'

'You did have something in your head, Micky, didn't you?' Nuala's eyelids remained stationary for a good half minute.

'Well ....' Micky sank onto his hunkers, hanging his head between his knees as if exhausted, but he was embarrassed. 'Your turn, Ben. Tell us what you think. You're sensible and English and ....'

Once again Ben waxed indignant. 'I'm not any more English than you are. My blood is Mum and Dad's blood and they're full Irish. I just happen to live in England because of Dad's work.'

'He's fooling,' said Aideen.

'Sorry,' said Micky, 'you know what I mean. English people don't go on so much about ghosts and fairies and banshees like they do here.'

'Mostly down in the country where we live, don't forget,' Ferna interrupted.

'Yes, mostly there but, just the same, Ben's more used to not having them about at all across the water.'

'I see what you mean.' Ben forgave him. 'Well, what I have in my head about Mac Alúishin isn't what any of you said, except you, Micky, in a sort of way, about him having to do with the sea. Remember last year when Brains nearly drowned himself with those enormous waves rolling him over and under in Millionaire's Pool, and we couldn't pull him out and, then, all of a sudden, there he was on top of that huge swell that rolled him right up onto the wall. I've always had a queer feeling about that.'

'You never said anything,' said Aideen. 'What kind of a queer feeling?'

'Nothing really sure — that's why I didn't say anything — just a feeling that the sea changed its mind about drowning Brains ... it felt sorry. Oh, I know how daft that sounds, but now I'm wondering ....'

'As the sea hasn't got a mind to change, you're wondering if Mac Alúishin had anything to do with it?' Brains' question full-stopped Ben. He carried on. 'You said he had frog flippers, Micky. Maybe he was snorkelling in the pool and, speaking as the person most concerned — it was *me* drowning, you know, near enough anyway — you've made me remember something I didn't know I knew until now. That day I was too pleased to be back on the wall alive to care how I got there. But *now* I distinctly remember how suddenly I felt all soft and warm, even though the waves were still tumbling me about, and then it was as if someone slid a cushiony surfboard under my back and tipped me onto *terra firma.*' He hastily translated the phrase for them. 'Dry land, that is.'

'I wish,' said Aideen, taking a deep breath, 'I wish someone had done the same for Declan and Fintan.'

At her next breath, she was racing along the folds of the fields, mindlessly discharging a furious energy and, mindlessly, the others followed without even a glance to locate the dozen odd ponies which, latterly, had taken to bunching together in wild gallops more reminiscent of prairie mustangs than children's pets, unnerving to timid walkers and jittery dogs. The children leapt from stone to stone up the rough trail, their hearts thudding like thundering hooves. At the crest of the headland, they paused to survey the glittering, faceted sea of many shifts and shades, steadying themselves for the next reckless plunge down the jaggedly stepped track which, half-way, broke into two- and three-feet drops of turns and twists. Aideen made the final jump to Roshín Rock's pebbly beach and squinted behind her, the sun fetching sparks from her eyes, seeing the turmoil in their faces unwinding now like her own. But still their blood ran hot.

'Not here?' she called.

'No. Keep going.'

'Millionaire's then,' she cried.

Across the small beach, through the sea's edge, they charged full-pelt, up and over the pinky-purple granite rocks to the narrow cliff path which wiggled and squirmed the ins-and-outs of every cove and spit of coast the whole way to Oisín, doubling the road length of four miles. They ignored the *'Dangerous Cliffs'* sign as usual. Only strangers who did not know the safe short cut heeded that. Always, on the right, the cliff dropped steeply to the rock-filled sea. A high stone wall bounded the left. Around the curve ahead lay the Cove of Purple Shells. The powdery dust of the path puffed upwards under their thumping feet. The other thumping took them unawares.

Aideen shouted and flung herself face down onto the narrow grass verge of the cliff path in sudden panic, guarding her head with upraised hands. Ben and Micky acted as swiftly, but Ferna, Nuala and Brains barely had time to thin their bodies flat against the wall.

No rider could rein in a horse at that speed or in such a place and the horseman did not try. He tore between them in a rush of air, a hand clutching his riding hat, his dark-green coat tails flying. 'HURROO-OO-OO!' he yelled at them, wildly.

Shocked, pale-faced, they stood up and stared after the horse and rider.

'I thought I was dead entirely!' Micky's language was more rural under stress. 'Who is that madman at all?'

Ben's breathing came unevenly. 'He's the same one we saw in Oisín this morning, going like crazy towards Scadeen.'

'Honestly!' Aideen was speechless.

'He could have had us over the cliff, you know,' Nuala said.

'But he'd have been over himself if he'd tried to stop. That's quod erat demonstrandum, QED, that is, Quite

Easily Done, well, more or less anyway ....' Brains saw Ferna's filthy look and stopped.

'He shouldn't be riding along here at all. *It's not allowed,*' she said, aggrieved. 'Just supposing I did that on my pony. Mum would kill me.'

'Do you know that horse?' Aideen asked Ferna, sharply. 'You know all the horses and ponies round about, even if you do only live here in the summer. It's not one of those in the fields, is it?'

'Look out!' Ben yelled.

'He's coming back!' Nuala shouted, her feet rooted to the path, paralysed.

'Get down. Get down, all of yiz,' roared Micky, throwing himself at Nuala, forcing her to the ground in a heap.

The horseman was bareheaded this time and, in terrifying close-up, they saw his flaxen hair curling close to his head (in stiffly whorled curls like pictures of the Greek gods) tapering down to a small neat beard, corn-coloured in the sun. His eyes were open so wide that they looked like glass marbles, sea green. The horse sprang, creamy tail lifting like spume from the sea, hooves retracted as neatly as plane wheels, clearing the huddled bodies cleanly.

Slowly getting to their feet, they watched the man and his mount tear around the curve in a scatter of small stones, a devil-may-care 'Hurroo-ooo-ooo-ooo' echoing endlessly in the depths of their ears.

4

Seal Watching

Brains had been right to insist that they go on to Whisky Cove. 'Swimming is therapeutic,' he had said. 'Calms the nerves. Look at us, we're shaking like jellies.'

Each and every one of the children's nerves stood upright like sentries on instant alert as they rounded the curves of the cliff path, tossing off T-shirts and shorts as they slithered down to the cove, revealing their swimsuit togs which double-dutied as underclothes all summer long. The sea lapped level with the top of the rough cement and gravel wall which helped the natural rocky circle of the Big Pool to imprison the tide. The stubby little pillar, their diving post, poked enticingly out above it. Not another soul was about, a rare state of perfection.

The children dived and swam or crawled about underwater as they always did, teasing the little flat fish that hid themselves on the sandy bottom into a flurry of fins, but the usual exuberance of their shrieks and calls and laughter was missing. Each practised a diving or swimming technique, treading water now and then to catch a breath, surprised to find themselves tired.

'The seals are in,' called Nuala, pointing.

'Warm weather.' Aideen watched the two sleek, dark heads bobbing in the water a few yards from the pool, their large eyes lustrous, their whiskers bristly.

The seals gazed fixedly at the children, ducking, surfacing, emerging sometimes nearer, sometimes further away, as the tide swiftly and subtly deepened to cover the wall to knee height, then to waist level, as Ferna demonstrated by standing up on it, one eye on the seals.

'They have been known to come into the pool, you know,' she said, a whit nervously. 'I'm getting out. Anyway, it must be pretty late by now.'

Ben swam to the beach for a time check. 'Come on,' he yelled, 'it's nearly six o'clock. We'd better get a move on or there'll be search parties out for us.'

Sea bathers worth their salt and scornful of mollycoddling towels (always drying off in the sun as they fished pools or clambered over rocks to the Needles or in and out of caves), the children charged up the cliff, clothes in hand, their swimming togs and bodies drying in the warm air. They took the shortest route via the Nun's Hole and the Lion's Head. There they halted, loath to part, yet strongly aware of a need to be at one with families more likely now to fret over lateness.

'Do we need to tell?' It was Micky who asked the question circling in everyone's head.

'No.' Swimming had helped Ferna, the decisive one, to make up her mind. 'If we tell, one of them would be bound to contact the Gardai to watch out for that lunatic rider. They might even stop us going off on our own, you never know. Anyway, we'll probably never see him again. OK?'

They agreed with her reasoning as one. 'We could say about the bird,' said Brains.

'Of course, we can say about *that*,' said Nuala.

'Tomorrow?' the question floated between them as they split apart.

'Tomorrow,' floated separately back.

Ben and Aideen sprinted for home, glimpsing two women's figures outlined against the lowering sun, hard by Far Hills cottage, hands shading their eyes from the glare, seeking. That Aunt Maddy should look so relieved gave the cousins a weak feeling.

'There you are, Aideen,' Maddy said, 'and Ben. Good.'

'Mum, you're wearing that super dress,' panted Aideen.

'And *I'm* all dressed up, Ben, in case you haven't noticed,' Riona laughed. 'We've decided to have One of Our Evenings. We're all going out to eat so you'd better hurry up, both of you, and get changed.'

When their mothers threw the adult world to the four winds during their time together, they were as eager for life as ever they had been when children themselves. Things happened whenever their mothers had One of Their Days, or One of Their Evenings: there never was any warning. That was half the fun of it, Ben thought, grinning in delight. One second everything was ordinary and then, bang, they were on a boat heading for the Isle of Man, or driving through the mountains to picnic at the Hell Fire Club, or at the old lead mine chimney at Cattygallagher, or taking an express train to Cork and back, not to mention fascinating hours at the airport watching the planes go by, museum and art gallery visits, or to see the shrivelled up mummies at St Michan's Church and, once, to whisper in the Cathedral where lay buried the man who wrote *Gulliver's Travels*, Jonathan Swift, although his grim and shining death mask made that hard to believe.

'Great!' said Ben.

'Where are we going?' asked Aideen.

'Oh, just Queen Maeve's,' Maddy answered, pretending to be casual, 'we've booked a table.'

'Wow!' said Ben.

'You've always said it costs the earth at Queen Maeve's,' said Aideen. 'Have we won the Lottery or something?'

Aunt Maddy winked a wicked eye at Ben. 'You haven't forgotten your mother's birthday is coming up shortly, have you? Well, we're just bringing it forward a bit and putting all our spare cash into the kitty, that's all.'

'It'll be bread-and-butter cake on the real birthday, though,' said Riona, but she did not seem to mind. She headed them towards the garden path, her short brown hair bouncing jauntily, shining clean.

'No washing needed by the looks of you,' added Maddy. 'That'll save time.' She turned to her sister. 'Come on, Ree. Let's do our make-up while they change. I can't wait to try out your mauve eye-shadow.'

~

Seated at the red check clothed table under the fishing nets and marker bobbles festooning down from the ceiling of Queen Maeve's restaurant, Ben peered about him in the greeny light filtering through the bottle glass windows.

'That's what's called atmosphere.' Aunt Riona winked discreetly, which made her eye-shadow gleam mysteriously as she surveyed the capstan, wheels, oars and anchors attached to the walls of this converted old boathouse.

Aunt Maddy fluttered curly black eyelashes at them across the yellow flame bubbling up from the fat red candle standing in the centre of the table. 'And it's so we can't see what's on the menu either. Anyway, I've left my glasses at home. You'll have to read the menu for me, Ree.'

A free-standing fish tank near their table magnetised Ben. Gigantic lobsters and crabs fumbled to and fro in the artificial setting, utterly baffled by the strange surroundings. Ben jabbed Aideen's ankle with the toe of his shoe, making her look.

'Poor things!' her voice rose high, indignant. She turned to her mother, aghast. 'Why are the poor things in a fish tank, Mum?'

Maddy regarded the imprisoned crabs and lobsters in dismay. 'Oh! Er ... Hum ...!'

'More atmosphere, that's what it is. Take no notice.' Riona's eyes never left the menu. 'Oyster soup .... Mmmmmmm. Ooh, Lobster salad ....'

At the next table, two jelly-bellied men were busily giving the waiter their order, making frequent gestures towards the fish tank. The waiter slipped his note pad into a pocket and took a sort of shrimping net from a hook beside the tank.

'He's taking that huge lobster out.' Ben was astonished. 'What's he doing that for?'

Riona closed the menu with a snap, suddenly aware. 'No shell fish for me, Maddy.'

'You don't mean ...?' Aideen's cheeks turned an odd shade in the green-filled light.

''Fraid so,' murmured Maddy. 'It *is* a fish food restaurant, you know.'

Grim faced, Ben reopened the fish shaped menu card. 'Fresh crab and lobster,' he read aloud.

Aideen glared at the fat men. 'Murderers!' she hissed.

'We could swap places,' said Maddy, 'then, at least, you needn't see so much.'

Their backs to the tank, Aideen and Ben's qualms vanished as they attacked their own meal with voracity, Ben shattering the waiter's finer feelings by demanding 'just ordinary fish and chips, please,' instead of the luxuriously sauced smoked salmon, Dover sole and halibut fillets chosen by the others. Afterwards he gaped wolfishly at each delectable offering on the Cold Table finalé to the meal. The waiter, wiser now, spooned a generous sample of each dessert onto the children's plates. The mountains of strawberry, coffee and chocolate gateaux, walnut mousse, fudge melba, guava split, and scoops of vanilla and raspberry ice-cream, plus dollops and dollops of cream almost, but not quite, bested their stomachs' capabilities.

Riona eyed them with apprehension when the meal was over and they were outside in the car park. 'Some exercise is definitely called for,' she said firmly, 'and fresh air. It's Thursday. What say we walk along the pier to watch the fishing boats come in?'

Ben felt better as they strode along the West Pier, huddling into his anorak against the keen evening breeze. 'I have to admit I do feel pretty full,' he muttered to Aideen.

'Some people always make pigs of themselves,' she grinned. 'I'm just nice.'

'You ate more than me.'

'I did not.' On her mischievous face the prim look always seemed unnatural.

They had to shout at each other above the noise of the caterpillar-tracked cranes poised on the very edge of the pier wall, at the same time watching where to put their feet amongst the trails of wire hawsers and ridges of hard dried mud. Lorries threaded paths for themselves (not too considerately) through the Thursday crowd of Dubliners coming out either to buy or catch their fish for Friday.

'Watch out!' Maddy jerked Ben's shoulder.

He retrieved his right foot just before a rope noose tightened about it.

'Nit-wit,' said Aideen.

'Who's ....'

'Stop arguing. Come and look over here,' called Riona, peering over the harbour's edge. 'Look at the depth of it. I'd hate to be that man over there.' She looked at the crane driver in his cab. 'The slightest mistake and over he goes — a drop of sixty feet or more it must be. They've done a good deal since we were here last, Maddy. There's a lot of road down there now, or are they cementing over the whole harbour bottom?'

She meant the concrete runway choc-a-bloc with mud-encrusted excavators surrounded by busy little dumper trucks.

'Look out, Mum!' Aideen yelled. 'That crane's swinging round.'

Two giant girders in its claws, the crane's jib swayed out from the pier's edge before unwinding vast lengths of cable to the reception committee of technicians far below.

'We're only getting in the way here,' Ben said. 'There's notices saying *"Danger!"* all over the place. Look — over there — and there.'

Maddy and Riona exchanged glances of guilt. 'You're dead right,' said Maddy. 'It's a lot safer further along where the boats are unloading.'

'There's a whole pile of them at it. Come on, Ben.' Aideen grabbed his arm.

Star of the Sea, Morning Star, Evening Star, Star of David, Star of Bethlehem, Star of Oisín, Daughter of Oisín, Son of Oisín ... the fishing smacks of many colours sailed into harbour, each trailed by screeching seagulls, wheeling, tumbling, diving after the fish gleanings cast overboard by feverishly working crews, gutting, sorting, boxing the trawlers' catch. Lorries on the jetties showered ice to the boats' decks the moment they tied up and the fishermen shovelled the ice into the fish boxes. Cranes lifted the boxes in nets to the waiting lorries, upon which men stood ready to stack them house-high amidst a confusion of shouts and yells. 'Left a bit, Mick. Up a bit. Down now. Down. *Down*, you eejit. Right there, Paddy, or you'll kill the man. Woah! Up! Stop! Are yiz deaf or what? Go on, now. Grand man yourself.' The lorries trundled off, headed for the next morning's fish market in the city, or inland to the country fishmongers. Refrigerated containers loaded too, bound for the late-night roll-on, roll-off ferry to Wales.

Just beyond the main jetty's hurly-burly, at the pier's extremity, anglers teetered on precarious rocks, the seawall and the wharf edge, flicking their rods back and forth, silver spinners flashing, hiding their triple hooks, tantalising the mackerel into a snap-and-grab raid that sealed its fate. Excited lines and hooks sometimes tangled, threatening the loss of an eye to innocent bystanders. Older anglers baited hooks for beginners, unknotted their lines, obviously remembering their own boyhood's breathless excitement. Ben never forgot the heavy thumping of his heart against his chest walls the first day he had held his very own sea rod. Wish I had it now, he half-grumbled to himself. Might have known we'd end up walking down here. Plucking the thought direct from his mind (she so often did this he hardly noticed), Aideen said: 'You're not in your smelly old jeans, so you couldn't anyway.' She nodded over his shoulder to someone, smiling. 'The cockle man and his dog are here, Ben, look.'

'Hello,' said the cockle man. 'Not fishing tonight?'

He always emptied out a pile of cockles from a salt-encrusted rucksack and used an ancient penknife to lever open the shells, often sharing the cockle meat bait with Ben, as well as giving several to his rough-looking, red-haired Irish terrier, forever trying to jaw and paw one open for himself.

'All dressed up tonight, are we? Very nice.' The man

admired Aideen's jade green jump-suit as her blazer blew open.

Aideen blushed a little. 'Oh, well, you know ... have you seen Micky or Ferna, or anyone?'

'None of your gang here that I've seen. Your friend Mr Carrigan's over there though, staring out to sea as usual. Never fishes, does he? Funny man.' He finished baiting and cast an expert line far out to sea.

'Ben! Aideen!' Riona's high-pitched call came in the wind.

'There she is. Over there.' Aideen saw her aunt standing with Maddy on the outskirts of a knot of people clustering above the flight of steep, deep-water stone steps, where dinghies and small craft dropped off passengers, or picked up sailing crew.

'I bet someone's caught something really *big*. Looks exciting. Come on.' Ben spoke to thin air. Aideen was already spring-jumping on her toes on the fringe of the small crowd.

'Here! Come over here.' By now Maddy and Riona had squeezed into a tiny space, gripping the protective railing. The children wriggled through. Now they could see.

A young seal rolled helplessly in each stir of water swirling from the passing trawlers, thud-thudding into the last half-submerged step with each swell. Aideen saw the deep slash in its side spill crimson into the sea. Her heart contracted. Ben was aghast. An instant thought flashed between them. Could this be one of the seals from Whisky Cove? The small bewildered face looked at them, a tear rolling from one eye. Sympathy sighed around the clutch of watchers. Ben gripped

Aideen's elbow so strongly she flinched, yet found comfort in it also. Riona saw their distress.

'But, look,' she cried to them, 'don't you see? It'll be safe in a minute or two. The net's quite near now.'

The children had not seen the length of orange trawling net being dragged through the water, an end held by men on either side of the jetty who, even as they held their breaths, curled the net into a hammock shape beneath the seal's body and lifted it clear of the sea. The little crowd broke apart, running to help the men haul the seal up on to the wharf.

'Someone fetch Mr Carrigan,' yelled a voice.

'That's the man for the seals all right,' nodded a fisherman beside Maddy.

'I'll get him — I saw him a minute ago.' Aideen whirled, but buffered to a dead stop against a very solid body.

Mr Carrigan's gentle hands moved her to Ben's side. 'Ah, Mrs Maddy,' he said, tipping the peak of his beloved old tram driver's hat with a courtly gesture, 'And Mrs Riona, too, no less. It's a grand evening after the bad day for us all — but, excuse me now, the little one there has need of me.'

The 'little one' was aiming frightened, sharp-toothed bites at his rescuers, not one daring to risk losing a finger by going too near.

'Ah, you poor little dear,' Mr Carrigan said. The snapping jaws closed into gentle nuzzling movements. Mr Carrigan examined the seal's wounds. 'Lost your way, have you? And no wonder.' His tufty eyebrows jerked meaningly at the harbour works in the background. 'Never mind. You come with me. I'll have you right in no time at all.' He scooped the seal into his arms and headed for his battered mini estate car. 'Open those doors for us, Ben, and spread out the old rug.' He laid the seal down with care. 'There now. Don't be crying anymore, young one. We'll soon have you home and well as can be.'

He wiped the seal's eyes with a ragged blue handkerchief. Not another tear fell.

5

Look-Out Cottage

Ben's uneasy sleep registered the shish-whish of early morning traffic passing by on the road outside the thick cottage walls of his bedroom. His watch flicked seven thirty. Mr Carrigan's bus would be crawling uphill from the station by now. He dived into his shorts and shirt. No doubt, Aideen and Maddy were sleeping like concrete in the room below, as usual; Aideen will be mad at me going out for news of the seal without her, he thought, but I have to know. Paddy Joe, the relief driver, was at the wheel, not Mr Carrigan at all.

'Mr Carrigan's having the morning off,' he told Ben. 'He phoned in late last night. Something very important came up, he said. It has to be something pretty big for Mr Carrigan to do that.' His slow wink hinted a need for secrecy. 'Of course, we did hear a bit of a rumour about a little hurt seal in the harbour last evening ... ye wouldn't know anything at all about that, would ye?'

'Well ....' Ben hesitated, unwilling to betray Mr Carrigan.

'Ah, sure, don't worry, boyo. Don't we all know about Mr Carrigan? And isn't he better than any vet when it comes to them little seal folk?' Paddy Joe throttled the engine and heaved at the gear stick. 'Maybe ye'll go on up to Mr Carrigan's place after your breakfast?' he shouted above the engine.

Disappointment dragged at Ben's insides as he watched the rackety old bus grind uphill. I suppose I'm still tired, he thought. There had been much talk last night, their tongues so loosened by good food and excitement that it had been midnight before his and Aideen's bedtime. Everything had come out: their deepest feelings about Fintan and Declan, the swimming and the seals in Whisky Cove, Mac Alúishin, and how he appeared differently in each of their heads.

'How do you see him, Mum?' Aideen had asked then, starting the swift to-ing and fro-ing of half thoughts, half sentences, the four of them called talking together.

'Me? Well ... I ... er ... um ...' mumbled Maddy.

'Go on,' urged Ben.

'Er ... well, you see ...'

'She means *we* only know about Mac Alúishin because of *you,*' explained Riona.

'Correct. Because he's real to *you*, he's become real to *us,*' said Maddy.

'What do you mean *real*? Of course he's *real*!' Aideen protested.

'You don't think we've just made him up! How can you make someone *up*?' asked Ben.

'Um ... no ... not *made* him up ....' Maddy hesitated.

'But children's imaginations can ... they can conjure up ... oh ... Maddy, you explain,' urged Riona.

'What she means is, if you all see something different, then he could be what's called a figment of the imagination — but I don't think he is.'

'No. Children often do see things, I mean, folk, that's to say, well, people, that adults can't,' said Riona.

'There you are then!' cried Aideen.

'See!' Ben exclaimed.

'But, Mum, *you* must have a picture of him, too. Tell us,' Aideen pleaded.

It was Riona who replied: 'I do, as a matter of fact. He's kind of wispy and shadowy, and *warm*, as if some kind of light glowed inside him. That sounds silly, doesn't it? But he's not, well, *solid*, as we are.'

'Good heavens, Ree, he's not like that at all. I know we've laughed about the children and Mac Alúishin and Flag o' the Woods ....'

'*Laughed*?' Ben was indignant.

'Not really laughed, enjoyed is more what she means,' explained Riona.

'Mm, that's right, enjoyed. Anyway, Mac Alúishin is the friendliest thing all out. He makes me feel the lot of you are safe as houses whenever he's around. But I *imagine* him as a sort of modern day Robin Goodfellow in T-shirt and jeans,' said Maddy.

A bubble of silence had encased all four of them then until Ben described the bird's flight from the old oak tree.

'You mean, you saw it too?' asked Riona.

'Extraordinary looking thing,' Maddy remarked.

'But neither of you said anything about it until now,' said Riona.

'Well, neither did you, Aunty,' Aideen pointed out.

'We distinctly thought you might be uneasy if you knew about it,' Maddy explained.

'Us? Honestly! But what do you think it *was*?' Aideen asked.

'Whereabouts did you see it anyway?' Ben wanted to know.

'It flew right over us,' said Maddy.

'We were sunbathing between Twin Rocks ....' said Riona.

'Right *overhead*.'

'Its wings clapped up and down like an, er, like a sheet flaps on the clothes line on a stormy day,' Riona remembered.

'Was it some kind of giant eagle, d'you think?' asked Ben.

'No, it wasn't an *eagle*.' Maddy was sure about that.

'What *was* it then — a heron, a pelican, a flamingo? A stork?' wondered Ben.

'Micky said it might be an albatross.' said Aideen.

'Well, I've never seen an albatross,' Riona told her.

'*No one* in this country has ever seen a real albatross,' added Maddy.

'Aideen said it could have escaped from the zoo.' suggested Ben.

'We thought of that.' Maddy answered.

'We rang the zoo, but there's nothing missing,' said Riona.

'It dropped right down into the sea, more *fell* than dropped, really,' Maddy recalled.

'Where the waves all foam together, you know, over towards the lighthouse,' said Riona.

'Disappeared. Right into the sea.'

'The foam.'

'I see,' said Aideen.

'Oh,' added Ben.

'Very odd,' continued Riona.

'Most peculiar,' Maddy agreed.

That conversation got us nowhere fast, thought Ben as he hopped down the cottage's garden path of stepping stones, brooding. No wonder I had queer dreams all night. He side-stepped to the small field gate, too rusted and shaky to open nowadays but good enough for leaning on. His face lifted to the sun. Hot already. Mm. Sleepy. Wake up, Aideen, he thought, drowsily, needing to share a foreboding that Mr Carrigan's absence roused in him. The small crying face of the seal haunted him.

It was a little while before he became fully aware of the helicopter's distant drone. He opened his eyes to see the distinctive yellow of the air/sea rescue chopper looping inwards from the bay. But the weather was fine. Practising? They never practised as early as this. It's coming direct for Roshín Rock. Oh, come on, Aideen, *wake up*. Impatience swept over him.

'Hi! I heard a chopper! What's it doing?' Aideen stood in the doorway, dressed but yawning, her hair uncombed and spiky.

Ben jumped, taken by surprise. 'You're up. Great. I don't know what it's doing but I'm dying to find out, and there's no news about the seal either. Mr Carrigan has the morning off.'

'Hey! Wait a sec. How d'you know he's got the morning off?'

He explained.

'You were mean going without me,' she scowled.

'How can I wake you without waking your Mum?' Ben asked. 'Anyway you're awake now, so come on. Let's find out what that chopper is up to.'

'I can't see it now. It must be right down over the water.'

'That's why I want to go over the top and see what's happening. Come *on*.'

She's still half asleep, he was thinking, even as she passed him at the run, bare feet flashing. He put on a spurt as they reached the craggiest part and climbed fast to the crest of the promontory, trying to ignore the jabs from his protesting knee.

There it was, the blades' downdraught flustering the calm sea into a flurry as it hovered, clacking, crawling sideways like an airborne crab, cautiously edging nearer to the cliff face. The tide was full, obliterating the tiny beach. A man sat in the wide side opening of the helicopter body, his legs dangling over its edge; he had binoculars raised to his eyes and was scanning every inch of cliff, shore and rock face. A ropeladder swung down from the helicopter to within a foot or two of the water.

'What on earth is he looking for? That's no practice,' said Ben.

'Well, whatever it is, he can't find it. Look. They're packing up,' said Aideen.

The man had put away his binoculars and was hauling in the ladder; the helicopter blades lifted the machine into a turning up-rise and a fast whirlaway. The observer gave one last glance downwards and saw them. He gave a thumbs-up sign and grinned widely, his teeth gleaming in the clear morning's sunlight.

'Whatever it was, it must be all right.' Aideen waved back to him.

'I'm starved,' said Ben. 'D'ye think breakfast's anywhere near ready?'

'Only one way to find out. It's your Mum's turn today, isn't it?'

'Slow down,' he said. 'My knee's playing up a bit, blooming thing.'

The fetching smell of frying bacon weakened Aideen's own knees as she climbed over the rickety iron gate. Maddy urgently beckoned to them through the window. 'News!' she called. In the kitchen the radio was going full blast.

'Sh! Sh!' Riona waved the cooking tongs at them. 'Listen,' she hissed, nodding towards the radio.

> And, finally, a further report from the Air Sea Rescue Service, which was alerted by early morning swimmers reporting distant viewings of a person, or persons, falling from the cliffs in the Roshín Rock region, at Ballydun. No casualties have been found. The aircrew are satisfied that the sightings were caused by refractions of light occasioned by the particularly brilliant weather conditions prevailing, a pleasant note upon which to end this news summary.

'Huh!' said Ben, astonished.

'We've just seen all that,' Aideen told her mother. 'He must have been radioing in that report while we were still there.'

'Who?' asked Maddy.

'The man with the binoculars, that's who.' Ben described the helicopter's manoeuvres, ending: 'It's all happening round here these last few days, isn't it? I mean there always seems to be something, ever since ....'

The four regarded one another in silence.

'Just coincidence,' murmured Maddy. 'Anyway, I'm glad no one did fall over the cliff. The last one who did was a very stupid woman trying to collect plant specimens.'

'She was rescued, though,' said Riona.

'Yes, with two broken legs,' said Aideen.

'And then there was the boy fishing off the Scadeen rocks,' said Ben. He never nagged to be allowed fish there now. That boy had slipped, and drowned.

'Refractions of light. I don't know too much about those. Have either of you done anything like that at school yet?' Maddy might be a brilliant ballet teacher but scientist she was not.

'Only sort of,' answered Ben. 'Anyway I can't think when I'm starving.'

Riona slid eggs, bacon and sausage on to every plate and heard about the missing Mr Carrigan between her son's large mouthfuls.

'You'd better run up there as soon as you've finished. On the other hand, maybe you'd better not.' Riona looked at her sister. 'The poor little seal might not still be ....'

Aideen jumped up, cutting that sentence in half. 'We'll wash up as soon as we get back, Mum, honestly. *Come on*, Ben, you must have drunk enough coffee by now.'

Half a mugful went down in one gulp. 'I'm ready.' Ben paused at the doorway, grinning. 'Don't worry, you two, I'll be back to peel the potatoes, as usual.'

Mr Carrigan's sparkling white cottage stood halfway up the purple-heathered slopes of East Mountain, at the extreme end of a muddy track spattered with deep potholes. 'It's not much of a mountain,' Mr Carrigan always said, 'but my windows look at the whole of Dublin Bay and beyond, and isn't that a very fine thing?'

'Look-Out Cottage' said the piece of driftwood nailed to an ivy-wrapped tree trunk beside the scrolled and patterned wrought-iron gate; this opened into a strange little garden where no flowers grew but where evergreen hedging was carved and shaved into fishy shapes which, here and there, seemed to swim above the sanded and gravelled ground below.

'You never told me he had a garden like this,' said Ben. 'It's the best garden I've seen in my life.'

'I didn't know either,' Aideen said. 'I knew where he lived but I've never been here before. I thought you knew that. But would you look at the gate!'

Ben gave it a cursory glance, more fascinated by the hedgy fish shapes. 'How about this one?'

'Look properly.' Aideen's forefinger traced an outline in the centre of the gate.

'It's a seal!' Ben looked at it in delight. Seen from inside the garden, the gate's motif stood out sharply against the sky. 'But you don't notice it from the lane. That's brilliant.'

'And would that be the one you're after coming about?'

Their startled about-turn seemed to amuse Mr Carrigan. He was standing in the lane, resting his elbows on the stone wall, chewing at the stem of a stubby pipe. 'You're too late for the other little fella,' he said.

They deflated like pricked balloons. Aideen breathed deeply. 'What do you mean too late, Mr Carrigan?'

'He means it's dead, that's what.' Ben looked utterly depressed.

'Hold on now, young feller-me-lad.' The pipe smoke curled up, tangling in Mr Carrigan's tufted eyebrows. 'Did I say any such thing?' he asked. 'I did not,' he answered himself, 'that little darlin's back where he belongs this very minute.' He read their faces.

'You're happy now, eh? That's the ticket.'

'But what about that bleeding wound all down its side? It can't swim like that, at least it couldn't last night.' That baffled Ben.

'Well, now, I'll show you. I knew right well you'd be worrying yourselves all night long and, like as not, you'd be out to my bus first thing this mornin'.'

'I was, too,' said Ben.

'Of course you were. Isn't that why I told Paddy Joe to drop you the hint about visiting me after your breakfast?' He paused. 'I'll tell you a secret, if you don't go blabbing it around.'

Aideen promised, instantly.

'Cross our hearts,' added Ben, drawing the sign across his chest.

'I've a little home movie camera but I don't go advertising the fact, seeing I'm not too handy with the thing. It'd be a bit of a joke to the other driver fellas, you know. Anyway, it's grand for keeping a record of my little patients.'

'Fabulous!' Ben's grin dazzled out.

'Come on in. I'll put on the fillim for you. It won't take me a minute.'

As the small projector was already set up, and black velvet curtains drawn across the window, switching on and focusing upon the white wall was instantaneous. 'I've fixed up a contraption that keeps the camera trigger down so that I can run round and be in the fillim myself,' explained Mr Carrigan, as he watched the film reel out scratchy flashes of light into the dark room until it steadied and cleared.

'There's the seal,' breathed Aideen.

'The two of you enjoy yourselves watching that now, and I'll be making a pot of tea for us for after.' He gave his crooked toothed grin at the children's absorption. 'Talking to myself I am.'

In the film, the seal had propped itself on its flippers, on the same table where their elbows rested now, intently watching Mr Carrigan thread a darning needle, holding it up to an angle-poised spotlight to do so. This done, he laid the needle on a tray at the end of the table which was covered in gleaming white plastic, and picked up a large scallop shell.

'It's like an operating theatre,' whispered Ben, with the authority of experience.

Mr Carrigan delved his fingers into the shell and thickly smeared the ointment it contained all around the seal's wound, talking all the while. Gradually the restive small body relaxed, became still, its eyes lifting to Mr Carrigan's, who stroked its head and nudging muzzle.

'I'd like to know what he's saying,' said Ben. 'I wish the film had a sound track.'

'I hope that ointment is some sort of anaesthetic,' Aideen muttered, flinching as Mr Carrigan pushed the needle into the deep wound's mouth and out again on the other side for the first stitch. 'It doesn't *seem* to feel a thing.'

'Probably like the jab I got for my knee, only that knocked me unconscious,' said Ben. 'That ointment stuff might have been better. I could've watched them doing my knee, then.'

'Ugh!' said Aideen, not raising her eyes from the needle.

Mr Carrigan smoothed out each jagged tear and re-joined it with the finest of needlework.

'Invisible mending,' she thought, admiring the skill.

'You can hardly see where it was. Better than mine even.' Ben checked his still livid scar.

'Now what's he doing? Oh, I see.' Aideen gazed, fascinated. Having taken a king-sized black plastic bag from under the table, Mr Carrigan was pulling from it wide strands of kelp and knotty wads of seaweed, which he used first to pad the wound and then to cushion the seal all about, creating a nest into which it huddled eagerly. Playful flippered gestures, flicks of snout and rolling of eyes all but embraced Mr Carrigan when he unwrapped a blue plastic bag from the depths of the black one.

'No wonder,' Ben grinned.

They watched the seal being fed with small, whole herrings, each one swallowed with a gulp-and-a-half motion.

'Mr Carrigan doesn't forget a thing, does he?' said Aideen.

'Ah, look. It's dropping off to sleep,' said Ben.

'And Mr Carrigan's walking out of the picture,' said

Aideen, 'he's probably going to ....'

'He's going to give you that tea he was talking about, that's what.'

Mr Carrigan's soft-footed entry made them jump. 'Well, and what did you think of all that?' he asked, putting down a tray, switching off the projector and going over to the window to pull back the curtains. Sunlight blinded in. They shielded their eyes against the glare.

'I think Paddy Joe's right,' said Ben. 'You're better than any vet with "them seal folk". That's what he said about you, you know.'

'Oh, he did, did he?' said Mr Carrigan. He poured tea into mugs of a deep cobalt blue, paler blue dolphins embossed around their sides.

'Where do you *get* so many fishy things?' Aideen asked.

'Ah, sure, people give them to me, you know. What about my teapot? D'ye like that?' Mr Carrigan lifted off the knitted cosy.

The teapot was shaped into a seal's body, the tail curving into a handle, and its open mouth was the spout. The recessed lid made a smooth body outline. The teapot also gleamed a deep cobalt blue.

'Oh, I'd love to own that.' Ben's envy leapt out.

'Drink up your tea now, the two of you, I'll have to be off to my bus pretty soon.'

'I thought you said you were no good with a movie camera, Mr Carrigan. That film was perfect. Wasn't it, Aideen?' Ben's spoon of sugar missed the mug and hit the table. 'I know you said the little seal was back home where he belongs, but how did he get back?'

'Same way as he got here, in Mr Carrigan's Mini van, how else? Isn't that right, Mr Carrigan?'

Mr Carrigan smiled at her. 'You're the sensible one, aren't you?'

'Are you sure the poor little fellow will be all right, though?' persisted Ben.

'Oh, ye can rest easy about that. The little darlin's in the right place now, right as rain he'll be. Drink up your tea.'

'*You* didn't cut those hedgy fish in the garden, did you, Mr Carrigan? Don't you have to be a, oh, I forget what it's called, to do that?' asked Aideen.

'A topiarist, you mean?' Mr Carrigan answered without hesitation. 'That's a little bit of a hobby I found for myself in my spare time. One summer I used to see a fella clipping and shaping peacocks and suchlike into a hedge as I'd be drivin' my bus alongside, and I thought, that's something I'd like to try my hand at, and so I did, and then I fetched a book or two out of the library to study it up ....'

'Is that your telescope?' Ben interrupted Mr Carrigan's eager flow, his eyes lured to a large telescope on a tripod, to the left of the window.

'Well, it's not my aunty's.' Mr Carrigan laughed aloud.

'You're rude, Ben,' expostulated Aideen.

'Ah, no, now. That he's not. He's just a bit taken with it, aren't I right, Ben?'

'I'd like to take it, you mean,' Ben retorted. 'It's a beauty. You must be able to see for miles with that.'

'Be it starlight or sunlight, don't I see all I need to see with it, young fella-me-lad.'

'Starlight. Do you know about stars and planets as well? You've got a lot of hobbies, Mr Carrigan.' Aideen's respect increased by the minute.

'You could say that.' Mr Carrigan piled the mugs onto the tray.

'The night sky? I suppose you'd never let us ....' Ben stopped short, remembering Aideen's 'rude' label.

But Mr Carrigan's face instantly wore the look of someone given a present. 'Ah, sure, why not indeed? Maybe your mammies wouldn't mind you staying up a bit late one of these nights? Coming near to midnight is the best time for things like that.'

Aideen sprang up. 'They'll let us come, I know they will. Let's go and ask them now, Ben.'

'Hold your horses there. Would you like a try-out look o' the telescope for a minute? Take turns now. Then I'll have to be off.'

Aideen saw to the very bottom of Whisky Cove's Big Pool before handing the telescope over to Ben. She was impressed.

Already Mr Carrigan was reaching out for his driver's cap. 'Be off with you now.'

'But what about this morning?' asked Ben, his eye still glued to the viewfinder, examining Kish lighthouse, eight miles out to sea.

'What about this morning?' said Mr Carrigan, sounding cagey.

'The helicopter,' said Aideen, 'and the radio saying someone was supposed to have fallen over the cliff.'

'We went to watch the chopper but they didn't find anything,' said Ben. 'You could have seen everything through this, couldn't you?'

'I suppose I could if I'd been looking.' Mr Carrigan covered the telescope with an old duster. 'Off home with you now.' He shut the door behind them. 'You can tell your Mammies about my fillim, and ask them about the star gazing, and tell them not to blab about things either. No one else is to know, mind that now.'

~

'The three monkeys!' said Ben. 'That's what he reminds me of.'

'Monkeys? Oh, the "Hear No Evil, See No Evil and Say No Evil" monkeys, do you mean?' Aideen widened her eyes at him. 'What on earth . . . ?'

'Well, Mr Carrigan sees everything through that telescope of his and he hears whatever news there is on the bus, but he doesn't exactly give away an awful lot himself, does he?'

6

The Russian Button

'All right?' Maddy shared out chunks of cheese, large green apples and a milk carton each. 'Now we're all free for the day.'

'Cold meat and salad, fruit jelly and ice-cream at six o'clock,' Riona announced, crisply. 'Baked potatoes for supper.' She and Ben exchanged smiles. He was addicted to baked potatoes.

'We might see you down at the cove later, you never can tell. I hope the seals come in today, especially Mr Carrigan's one,' said Maddy. 'I wish I didn't have to take my city class. Still, Ree's driving me in. We're killing about six birds with one stone as usual.'

Riona groaned. 'Shopping. Ugh. It cuts down on petrol anyway, and I can change my books and records at the library in town. I suppose you two will be with the others?'

'We will,' Aideen said.

'Take care, then. Don't do anything silly, either of you,' said Maddy.

Accepting the usual lightweight kisses of benediction, the children noticed anxiety flicker across their mothers' faces.

'Don't worry,' Ben said, 'Everything should be just ordinary today.' He picked up the plastic margarine box of picnic rations.

The day stopped being ordinary in no time flat, shortly after Brian's arrival, in fact; they had given him up, and Mac Alúishin too, no one having felt his presence, and were about to lower the white flag signal of occupation. Brains was relieved to find them still there. He took a battered file-index card from the back pocket of his jeans.

'Dad and me consulted a whole load of books in the library last night to identify that bird,' he began. 'There were piles of peculiar ones it could have been, except they're either extinct, or only in Asia or Australia, or somewhere like that and, as nothing has escaped from the zoo, Dad said it *had* to be a grey heron, it couldn't be anything else. He's a bird spotter you know. Anyway I've copied out the most important identification data.'

They sighed. If Big Brains, as they called his father, a university professor of archival studies, a subject so dull its meaning never sank in despite frequent efforts by Brains to spell out its purpose to them, if *he* had decided what kind of bird it was, that, they supposed, had to be that.

'Adult birds may achieve a length of over three feet.' (If Brains' index card was crumpled, his notes sounded smooth.) 'Blue-grey in colour with a whitish front. The beak is yellow and awl-shaped. The wings which carry dark tips move with a peculiar and unmistakable beat.

The legs are elongated in flight with the long neck held in an S-curve. Their nests are large and clumsily built of sticks, usually in a tree but occasionally on cliff tops. Herons nest communally in heronries, which may remain in use for centuries.'

'Centuries? You've got to be kidding.' Micky looked askance.

'No, honestly, Micky, that's what the book says.'

'Communal? Well, that's wrong for starters,' said Ben. 'I'd like to see more than one of those birds squeeze themselves into our tree.'

'A large nest of sticks, huh?' Micky grinned. 'That's the clue we need.' He jumped up. 'Come and watch Micky, the intrepid heron's nest investigator, at work. No, Ben, you might be a better climber than me but your knee's still a bit wonky.'

Ben could not argue about that. 'It's an awkward tree though, Micky, just bare trunk, dead branches, and all that funny stuff in a heap on the top. You'd better watch it.'

With a leg-up from Aideen to Ben's shoulders, Micky reached the first bare branch, and shinned haphazardly upwards until his head thumped into the tree's mobcap.

'It's pretty solid,' he shouted down. 'I'll try to wriggle into it from the middle.'

'Mind yourself, Micky O'Mara,' yelled Ferna, overcome by an unusual sisterly anxiety upon seeing nothing of him but legs, which spasmed out of view even as she shouted at him.

The oak tree's bushlike topknot rustled and crackled as it had yesterday before the bird flew out but, now, Micky's gasps and pants came through the shrouding greenery as his weight tipped the treetop ominously aslant. One leg stabbed through the strangling ivy creepers into thin air. A horrified intake of breath hissed from the rubber-necking group in the field. The leg withdrew. The leafy crown steadied.

'OK. I'm coming down.'

'His voice sounds peculiar.' Nuala's eyelids showed unease.

'Not to worry. Here he comes.' Ben shouted directions to Micky. 'Right foot over a bit more to the right. Feel for the branch there. That's it. Now left foot. There's a sort of hole straight down under it. Another inch or so. Got it? Good. Now the right again.' And so on.

The return down the barkless tree proved more trouble than the upward climb. Until Micky fell the last five feet only Ben's voice could be heard, but the moment her shattered brother rose to his feet, Ferna broke into a volley of abuse.

'Scaring us like that, Micky O'Mara. What are you *doing*, hanging your legs out like that? Look at your jeans. There's huge tears in them everywhere. Granny'll go *mad*, and you nearly fell out of the tree altogether. You want your head examined, you do ....'

Nuala's nudge halted her. 'Don't you think he's a horrible colour, your brother? Maybe you'd better shut up for a bit, Ferna.'

Aideen, Ben and Brains stared at Micky's pale, disquieted face. He's had a real scare, Aideen thought.

'Was it a heron's nest, or not, Micky?' She used a casual voice to calm him. 'Don't tell us you found an egg in it?'

'No.' Micky spoke in jerks. 'There's no egg, and no

nest either, only a sort of, well, a cushiony little platform kind of thing. It's quite comfortable, as a matter of fact, if you don't put your foot through, I mean, lots of raggy old cloths and hay and leaves mixed up together, kind of a little tree-house really.'

Brains' face fell. 'Dad's gone wrong somewhere. Wait until I tell him tonight.'

'So we're just as wise as we were before,' muttered Ben. 'Less really.'

'I did find something.' Micky felt in his pocket and withdrew a folded hand. He unrolled his fingers, watching their alert eyes. A brass button lay on his palm, backed by a shred of torn blue denim. Embossed on the button was a hammer and sickle.

Recognition hit them like a blow. Each face became white. The button souvenir Declan's father had picked up when the Wall came down in Berlin.

'Declan's Russian Button!' Nuala named their shock.

Brains examined it with care. 'It's *bona fide* all right,' he muttered to himself, 'Genuine, that is.' His words dropped into the silence like pellets. 'This is going to take quite a bit of digesting.'

Brains was right again. It was easier to digest their various provisions of cheese, cold sausages, hard-boiled eggs, tomatoes, cucumber, buttered crackers, chocolate biscuits, apples, oranges, milk and coffee to the last drop and crumb. Their appetites were sharpened by repeated dives and dips into the Big Pool.

'We never will know how the Russian Button got there.' Ben summed up hours of wondering, guessing and discussion. 'The most likely is what Ferna said on the way here. Declan must have climbed the tree sometime and the button tore off his jeans.' They all look as shaky as I feel, he thought.

'You'd think he'd have *said,*' murmured Nuala, for the umpteenth time.

'Or Fintan. They never did anything like that by themselves. And,' Aideen laughed a little, 'if Declan lost that precious button of his the whole of Oisín would have had to know about it.'

'What's the use of rabbiting on and on and on?' Micky turned himself on to his stomach and hammered his head up and down on his crossed forearms. 'We'll never know for sure. Ben's right.' His closed eyelids were tight and stiff.

Nuala sat on her hunkers. 'It's gone awful cold,' she said.

Ferna looked out to sea. 'Sea mist! That's all we need.'

The worst kind of sea mist was rolling towards them in black and gloomy swirls, wiping out all sunshine and warmth in seconds, covering them in a dank blanket instead. Shivering, they pulled their clothes on and took shelter in the small cave.

'I've a few matches in my jeans. We could light a fire,' said Micky, ready for action.

'Great man yourself, Micky. Let's grab all the driftwood around,' said Ben. 'Get lots of small dry bits to start it.'

Picnic wrappings tindered the dry sticks, and careful feeding of progressively larger pieces of driftwood soon turned it to a warm blaze. They knew the mist could clear as quickly as it came, although the foghorn's hoarse braying reverberated inside their ears. Not a good sign usually.

'Oh, fizzle,' said Brains, 'I think I've left Declan's button on that bit of rock shelf near the pool.'

'Where you put it for safety, I suppose?' Ben was sarcastic. 'Well, the tide's coming in so you'd better go and get it, hadn't you? Sometimes you're about as brainy as my left foot.'

'Sorry,' Brains said, humbly. 'I'll go this minute.'

He shuffled off into the murky mist, his hands outstretched, feeling for familiar rock shapes. They heard his feet trudging through the shale to the concrete wallway bounding the small Banana Pool. Then there was only the slip and slop of the unseen tide's smooth advance. Suddenly, louder, broken splashing began.

'He wouldn't be stupid enough to get into the pool in this, would he?' Ferna looked at Micky in accusation. 'I hope you remember Mrs Boffin expects us to look after Brains.'

'Of course he wouldn't swim in this. Don't be such an eejit,' said Micky.

'Sh!' Ben silenced them. 'There's someone else there. Listen!'

Aideen's face lit up. 'The seals are in. That's them, barking and grunting. They sound excited about something. Maybe lots of sprats and mackerel are coming in close with the mist, like they do sometimes.'

'D'ye think Mr Carrigan's seal is there?' Ben shared Aideen's delight. 'I wonder if Brains can see them?'

'Oh, gosh, I'd forgotten him again. Hey, Brains!' Micky yelled at the top of his voice, taking his neighbourly duties seriously at last.

Barks like hiccups, the slap of flippers beating the water and the crisp splashes of diving bodies blotted out

Brains' reply, if there was one. The seals sounded frolicsome.

'Probably can't hear us with all that. Let's all shout,' said Ben.

'Brains!' they called. *'Bray-ens!'*

The splashing and barking ceased. Instead, a pathetic wail mixed with the faraway moo-ing of the Cow and Calf foghorns, blowing now at longer intervals. The dank fog-fuzz began unwinding from the beach, preparing to spread upwards to the Hill's peak. Out of the thinning mist, a wraithlike figure came.

'Got it OK?' Ben asked Brains, disguising the relief he felt at seeing his small friend.

'No, I did not get it.' The adam's apple in Brains' throat rose and fell like a mini elevator. 'I think those blooming seals must have knocked it into the water with their cavorting. One bumped right into me.' He swallowed again. 'Quite gently though.'

'Glad to be back on *"terra firma"*, are we?' Micky's joke was gentle. For once.

'Hark at him,' Nuala said.

'Learns something every five years, you know.' Ferna leered at her brother and dodged the mock blow he aimed at her.

'Watch it,' he growled.

'You two O'Maras,' said Aideen. 'Stop it, will you. Look, the sun's breaking through. It'll be clear in a few minutes. We can go and do a proper search.'

Micky spat onto the glass of his diving goggles and smeared it about in a professional manner before positioning them over his eyes. 'Where are my flippers?' He cast about among the rocks. 'I left them here somewhere. Hah. There they are.' He pushed his foot inside one, struggling to pull the stiff rubber strap over his heel. 'I'll dive and look for it, it's bound to have fallen into the water.'

'We *all* will. Since you got all that snorkelling gear you think ....'

'Stop niggling him, Ferna,' said Nuala, 'just because he's your brother. Micky's all right, you know.'

Micky gazed at her reddening face and waited for her eyelids to re-open. He felt very grateful, and surprised. 'Thanks, Nuala,' he said.

'Hurry up,' she said, smiling, 'the others will find the Russian Button first, if you don't.'

He splay-footed after her, the flippers awkward on land, but as soon as he threw his body into the water lapping the beach he finned away with fishlike suppleness. The sun shone out, colouring the water aquamarine, reflecting the hue of the sky and the fluorescent cloud fluffs. Micky curved towards the Big Pool, circling the Russian Button's last known resting place. He gulped air, gripped the snorkel's mouthpiece between his teeth, uptailed his body underwater and swam fast. He planned a surprise arrival under their very noses.

A light slap tapped the back of his neck, followed by a quick, light flick across his shoulder blades. He sucked air through the snorkel. He would dive under whatever it was, seaweed probably. The water shone in front of him. He was conscious of a tickling movement along the length of his spine, as if a small hovercraft synchronised its progress to his.

What on earth? He revolved, looked up.

The seal's smooth body floated on the surface above

him, its flippers weaving in slow motion. A golden gleam sparkled at each downward stroke of the left flipper. Micky blinked to clear his eyes, not believing that he saw Declan's Russian Button embedded between the finger bones of that flipper. His gasp sent bubbles of air effervescing through the water, at which the seal wriggled away, disclosing a thin line of black stitching down one side. Micky power-kicked upwards, his lungs bursting. He surfaced beside the wall.

'Hey! Where've you been?' Aideen's fury was real. 'Are you trying to frighten us to death or something? Nuala said you were coming ages ago.'

'We kept shouting at you to watch out for the seals,' said Brains.

'I've seen one,' panted Micky, 'in close-up, you'll never believe ....'

'What? What'll we never believe?' snapped Aideen.

'Take your time,' Ben said more kindly, watching Micky drag off his goggles. 'You're puffed.'

'Declan's Russian Button! I've seen it, Aideen,' Micky gasped.

'Where? All right, I'm sorry I yelled. Where did you see it?'

'We've looked and looked,' said Nuala, 'and the water's so clear we could see right to the bottom.'

'It's not ... on ... the ... bottom!'

Well, stuck on a rock, or wherever, silly,' said Ferna.

'Not on a rock ... on a *flipper*.'

'Stop kidding, Micky O'Mara.'

'Cross my heart. *It's on your seal's flipper, Aideen*.'

'*Look*,' cried Nuala. 'They're there again. Look!'

Micky jerked himself up, and onto the wall. Barely

ten yards off, a snorting seal ejected from the water almost to its tail end, his flippers like torpedo fins. The little ladder of black stitches on its body was clear and the sun winkled out a glint of gold from the tip of one flipper.

'You're right,' breathed Ben.

'Of course I'm right,' Micky said.

7

Half a Brother

Riona's speciality whistle shrilled from the cliff top at the bend above the Needles. Maddy's arms semaphored to the children, pointing to the Isle of Man ferry boat shaving past Whisky Cove's outer edge, sailing in a cheeky flurry of water like a toy boat in a bath tub. When it was abreast of the Big Pool it seemed near enough to touch. It was their delight to scream out greetings to the passengers crowding the decks, who stared at them, waving, envious. I bet the seals hate the ferry's engine noise, thought Aideen today, looking to see their reaction, but the seals had vanished. Maddy and Riona reached the beach, pulling clothes over their heads, to reveal bikinis at the ready.

'Make way, we're coming in,' cried Maddy. 'Town was roasting. Our clothes feel all sticky and revolting.' She threw down her cotton dress and raced Riona into the sea from the open beach; they emerged seconds later, arms and legs beating out a smooth fast rhythm. Riona grabbed the wall of the pool in half a minute and

Maddy wiped her eyes clear of water a second afterwards.

'Do you fancy a trip on her?' said Riona.

'Did you see the seals, Mum?' said Ben.

'Mr Carrigan's seal, would you believe,' said Aideen.

Brains butted in. *'It had Declan's Russian Button.'*

'What did you say?' Riona said to Ben.

'What's that about a button?' Maddy to Brains.

'What d'ye mean a trip on her? Who?' Ben to Riona.

Questions criss-crossed, needed untangling. Aideen described the discovery of Declan's Russian Button in the oak tree, its loss, and magical reappearance on the flipper of Mr Carrigan's seal.

'No one would believe it!' Riona.

'There's more things in heaven and earth ... er, um, I can't remember the rest, but you know what I mean.' Maddy.

'You mean "There are more things in heaven and earth, Horatio, than are dreamt of in your philosophy", that's from *Hamlet*, you know, Shakespeare,' said Brains.

Maddy raised one elegant eyebrow. 'Oh! Mm. Yes. Well, anyway ....'

'*I* think it's perfect,' said Riona. 'Declan himself couldn't think of a better person, well, er, creature, to have his Russian Button, now could he?' She smiled all round her.

A satisfied sigh lifted each child's chest as they let their bodies float in the deep water alongside the wall. Ben and Aideen helped their mothers up to join them.

'What exactly did you say about a trip, Aunt Maddy?' asked Ben.

'We were stuck in a traffic jam outside a travel agent's window this morning when we saw this cheap Day Return offer in the window — there and back for half nothing — so we're going,' grinned Maddy.

'Tomorrow!' said Riona.

Ben fell backwards into the pool. Aideen threw her arms about Maddy, whereupon they overbalanced into the water in a duet of shrieks.

Riona stood alone, dignified, until Ben grabbed her by the ankle. Her splashdown shuddered the whole pool. Nuala, Micky, Ferna and Brains swam over to investigate, sensing the unusual. News of the day trip voyage to the Isle of Man and back electrified them. As one, they abandoned Whisky Cove and sped homewards to bring notice of this day excursion offer to their families without delay.

'Tell your mothers, and your Granny, Ferna and Micky, that we'll be responsible for you, if they don't want to come themselves,' yelled Riona to their departing backs. She spread her towel on the warm shale and sank beside her sister. 'Everything's gone all quiet, Ree. Mm. Bliss.'

'Lucky you missed the mist,' grinned Ben, rather liking his pun.

'Mist. What mist?' Maddy was surprised.

'Oh, one of those come-and-go ones, you know — freezing, foghorns going, the lot.'

'We've only just got back from town,' said Riona. 'but we saw no sign of it on the way — I mean, you can always see if there's mist on the Hill on the coast road from town.'

'Oh, we were probably too busy nattering to notice,

Ree. Anyway, I'm glad we missed it.' Maddy lay flat, yawning. 'I want my forty winks in the sun,' she mumbled, drowsily. 'Wake me round five thirty, Ben, if you want to eat on time.'

Ben and Aideen regarded their mothers' carefree bodies kindly. His watch clicked 2.15 p.m. The usual afternoon influx to Whisky Cove was underway: toddlers in the care of au pair girls of every nationality, dogs with lolling tongues, barking and yelping with glee as they dashed in and out of the water, scattering sandy shale over picnics, their paws digging for a dropped stick or stone which sank deeper and deeper. Older children filled the Big Pool, showing off, shouting, banishing younger brothers and sisters to Banana Pool safety; adults squeezed into rock clefts, hot as ovens, or chose a rock-face with just the right slope to lean against for a long, long read of the paperback books protruding from picnic bags and baskets.

The children always tried not to resent the intrusion, even pitying the townies from suburban estates ringing Dublin city, but neither Aideen or Ben ever wished to stay with them. They either paddled the secret way to Millionaire's Pool, if the tide was out, or up to the cliff path to the hidden, slither-down trail, if it was in. Now they spreadeagled their limbs on the grassy hump overlooking the rock pool of emerald water. Only dead centre did the sandy floor gleam, the rest of it obscured by glossy brown seaweeds and limpet encrusted rocks, a difficult pool to get into and out of, except when full to the brim and safe for diving. One day they had seen a three-foot-long conger eel writhe across the sandy centre and into the seaweed darkness. Ben remembered

Fintan laughing when he said: 'Conger eels don't have a very good press around here.' He had enlarged upon that, aided and abetted by Declan, telling tall tales about fingers and thumbs lost to conger eels by local men and boys. 'The eels hold on forever, like a bulldog,' Declan had said, 'there's only one way to make them let go. You have to cut off their heads.' The Terrible Twins liked to leg-pull and exaggerate, Aideen knew, but always thereafter she would scan the depths of Millionaire's Pool with fearful care before diving in. They had never seen another eel. Ben's closed eyes and closed face told her he was still probing the mystery of Declan's Russian Button. She poked his ribs.

'What d'you think?' she asked him.

'I don't know what to think, do you? But it is sort of good about the seal having it.'

'Only for a while, I'd say. It will have to fall off sometime, I suppose. I love Mr Carrigan's little seal, Ben, don't you?'

'Yes,' he smiled. 'I do. He's the cutest thing all out, though I think we should give him a name instead of calling him Mr Carrigan's seal all the time.'

'Button!' she announced. 'That's what we could call him.'

'Dead right, Aideen. Button. That's really good.' He took a long breath. 'It would be even better if *they* knew.'

'Ah, sure, maybe they do.' A quiet voice rose from a portion of the pool hidden from their view by the overhang of rock below them. They thrust their heads and shoulders over the edge, startled.

'Mr Carrigan,' Aideen gasped, 'I thought you were driving your bus.'

'Gosh,' Ben said, 'you mean you've been down there all the time?'

'Well, No and Yes. The No meaning I'm not Mr Carrigan at all, and the Yes that I have been here all the time.' The man's grin displayed a set of perfect, pearly teeth. 'But just so ye won't be flummoxed entirely, I'll tell ye that Mr Carrigan and myself are brothers.'

'I didn't know Mr Carrigan had a brother,' said Aideen.

'Ah, well, ye can't know everything and I'm not around the Hill as much as himself.'

'Where do *you* live, Mr Carr ... oh, wait a tick, do you mean you are not called Carrigan? I don't get it.' Ben was blunt.

'We're what ye might call half-brothers, one different parent ye see. Kinseely's my own name. And where do I live? Well, most of my time is spent at sea, so to speak.'

'Sea fishing, d'ye mean?' asked Ben.

'Ye could say that,' Mr Kinseely winked a sparkling green eye, 'though I'm under the water more often than up on the top of it.'

'A *diver*?' Ben examined Mr Kinseely with interest. 'Sub-aqua, or deep-sea?'

'A bit of both, ye might say.'

He's not in the least like Mr Carrigan when you look at him carefully, Aideen thought. His eyes are a very shiny green for one thing, not blue, and his hair's longer. It would be really blonde if it wasn't wet and sticking to his head. Something about him tickled the back of her mind.

'Satisfied?' Mr Kinseely flicked water up at them in a shower of icy droplets. 'Are ye coming into the pool or are ye going to stay there gasbagging all day?'

'In!' Aideen lowered her legs into the seaweed fronds at the pool's edge, squirrelled about with her heels for the tiny rock shelf she knew was there, and flopped forward in a bellyflop dive.

Ben's entrance was even more ungainly. He spat out water. 'Where's Mr Kinseely?' he gasped.

'Right behind ye, me lad.'

They watched Mr Kinseely submerge below the surface again, without a sound, without a ripple. Ben took a deep breath and floated, face down, scanning the deeps, blurry-eyed. All he could see was seaweed and Aideen's legs treading water. He came up for air.

'Where is he, Aideen?' he called.

'Here.' Mr Kinseely emerged between them.

'Well, you weren't there a second ago,' said Ben, aggrieved. 'I was looking everywhichway, so I was, and the water is crystal clear.'

'I tried too, as a matter of fact, and I didn't see you either, Mr Kinseely,' Aideen sounded mystified. She was even more surprised now that she was so close to him that she could see his pale-gold, all-over tan shine phosphorescent against the green of the sea. I'd like my teeth to be as glistery as his, she thought — maybe he uses that Pearl Drops stuff on the TV ad. What's that he's saying?

Mr Kinseely repeated himself for her. 'I was saying, it'd be no harm for the two o' ye to learn a few tricks of me trade, no harm at all.' He frowned a bit. 'Them two young fellas of yours thought they knew it all, but they didn't, did they? They should've let me teach them before ....'

'Oh, you knew them too, did you?' interrupted Ben.

'Certainly, I did. Who didn't know the two of them? Ben, come on, now. If ye do what I tell ye, the roughest of seas won't frighten ye into a panic. It's the panic that does it, ye see. Mind you, they'd no chance at all once they'd had a crack off the rocks, and then they hadn't learned how to use storm waves.'

The children hung on his words.

'I'd like to learn,' Ben said.

Mr Kinseely grinned. 'That's the ticket, as me brother likes to say. Ye can start by changing the way ye got yourself into this pool a minute since.'

'But it's not deep enough for diving just now.' Aideen defended their clumsiness. 'You can't see the rocks properly with the seaweed.'

'There's diving and there's diving,' he replied, lifting himself on to a rock with smooth ease. On it, however, his movements became awkward.

'I'll do the safe dive for these conditions for ye. Watch me now.'

He launched his body like a glider and inserted rather than plunged it into a horizontal line a foot below the surface. No splash. Not even a ripple.

The children exchanged wry expressions. Mr Kinseely was expecting a lot if he thought they could do that. Mr Kinseely did expect them so to do. What is more, his method of instruction instilled confidence into their own bodies, eliminating fear from their minds. Within minutes, they were able to judge the angle of dive, skimming a safe twelve inches below water, another twelve above underwater hazards. Mr Kinseely doubled their lungs' oxygen intake and retention, using his system of breath control. Their usual gasps and puffs diminished into soft sighs and soughs.

'And we thought we could swim underwater before!' exclaimed Ben, after a Mr Kinseely-guided sub-aqua tour of the pool.

'I'm not afraid of getting caught in the seaweed any more either,' said Aideen, with satisfaction. 'It's really quite easy swimming through it just finning my feet and not moving my arms at all.'

'What about conger eels?' Ben thought Mr Kinseely would know for sure.

'Sure they'll leave ye alone if ye don't be annoying them,' said Mr Kinseely. 'It's fish they're after, not the likes of ye. Come on now, there's more for ye to learn yet.'

'We're nearly as good as Micky with his snorkel,' said Aideen with glee.

'I've seen the boyo,' said Mr Kinseely. 'He's good with that thing in his mouth all right, but how is he without it, tell me that? Ye are learning the right way. Ye can't always have them snorkel things handy, nor them floppy shoe things.'

'Flippers,' said Ben.

'Flippers, ye call them? Did ye ever! Well, lad, ye can't always have them in your pocket. Supposing ye fell out of a boat, or something similar? Anyway, I'd think the snorkelly thing would be no good at all with the waves o' the sea tipping water down the little hole and into ye.'

'Wait till I tell Micky that.'

'So ye can, lad.'

'You'll have to tell him, Mr Kinseely,' said Aideen, 'he'll never believe us. Are you going to be here tomorrow?'

'Not tomorrow,' Ben hissed, 'Isle of Man boat trip!'

'Oh, gosh, yes, the day after tomorrow, I mean.'

'The Isle of Man boat? Ye're not going on that thing, surely?' Mr Kinseely's eyes had gone a glacial green.

'I ... er ... yes, we're going to be on it tomorrow. Our Mums are taking us. It's a special day trip offer ....' Ben's voice trailed into the thin air, filling the space where Mr Kinseely had been. That man had expelled his body over the wall and into the sea beyond in one acrobatic leap, instantly submerging out of sight. Nor did he resurface.

'He seemed upset,' Ben said after some time had passed. 'D'ye think he's coming back?'

'No, probably not. I don't see his clothes anywhere. He must have left them further along. He went mad the minute we said about the Isle of Man ferry, didn't he?'

They continued to wait and worked hard to perfect the techniques they had just learned, but Mr Kinseely did not come back. In time, Ben's stomach clock alarmed, demanding nourishment.

'We'd better go and wake our Mums up,' he muttered.

'They'll be surprised about Mr Kinseely,' said Aideen.

8

Half a Voyage

'I did hear about Mr Carrigan having a mysterious brother, once or twice,' Maddy said, not unduly surprised, 'you know — when people wink and tap their heads or their noses, meaning there's something a bit peculiar, or a skeleton of some sort rattling about in the family cupboard. Just the same, I am glad he's taught you all those safe swimming techniques.'

'Me too, I call that a very good thing,' Riona murmured. 'Maybe he's an oil-rig diver, or some such, so he would be away most of the time.'

'Earning piles of money,' laughed Maddy.

After the evening meal and washing of dishes Ben said that he was off to the library. 'I need a load of books on scuba diving and deep-sea, and one about the Isle of Man. Don't you want another of that Susan Cooper series, Aideen?'

'Yes, I do. I can't wait to read the next one after *Greenwitch*. That was brilliant.'

'If you're going over to Oisín, you can go up the West

Pier and buy some fish for tomorrow night. We'll be out all day, remember. Get it last thing so it'll stay fresh. Take the coolbag, in fact, then it can go straight into the fridge.' Maddy handed her purse to Aideen. 'You'll have enough there for a good chunk of cod each, or plaice, if you like.'

'And don't forget you've to be home and in bed by ten o'clock,' Riona said. 'We have to be up early to catch the Isle of Man boat, remember.'

'We're not going to forget that.' Ben had a large grin pinned to his face.

Aideen hesitated. 'D'ye think any of the others might phone to say they're coming, Mum?'

'If they do, we'll arrange all the details. Don't worry about a thing,' said Maddy. 'Off with you.'

Aideen was lucky. The next two of the Susan Cooper 'Dark is Rising' series were waiting for her on the shelves of the pocket-sized library. She snuggled into a comfortable chair and began to read, lost to her surroundings. Ben's search was long-winded but at length he located a beginners' manual on scuba diving with an easy text and clear illustrations, but the book outlining the work of deep-sea oil-rig divers was a lot more difficult. The librarian promised to find a better one for him in a day or two.

New leaflets on display at the check-out desk dealt with the harbour's redevelopment. The librarian gave them a couple to take home. 'There's an extra large blast due in half an hour,' he told the last few readers in the library. 'By floodlight. Should be quite a sight, if you like the mess they're making of the harbour.' His eyes turned towards the ceiling in disgust.

'By floodlight?' Aideen stopped reading, surprised. Time vanished in a library. It was nearly nine o'clock and the dusky August evening had already coated the harbour with twilight. They locked their bicycles to the station railings and dawdled up the West Pier to the fish merchant with the sliding blue doors. He often threw in an extra fish. 'And one for the cat!' he would laugh, never asking if they had a cat at all. Aideen put the plaice fillets in the coolbag and zipped it tight. Twilight deepened to a velvety darkness now, except where gold pools of light encircled each pierside lamp.

'Now, that's done,' said Ben, 'we could watch the big blow-up the librarian talked about. We've time enough. Agreed?'

'Agreed,' said Aideen.

They mingled themselves into the crowd looking down to the dried-out reconstruction depths below the pier's edge. The most dangerous area had been roped off by the Harbour Police.

'We won't see much,' protested Ben.

The siren sounded, long and earpiercing.

'Clear the area!' shouted the police through loudhailers, halting all cars, turning them back to the sea front road. 'The rest of you stand against the wall over there.' The people pressing against the rope barrier shuffled backwards, reluctantly, the children squashed in their midst.

Ker-ump! Ker-ump! Ker-ump! Crack!

Every manjack of them clapped hands to their ears, dazed, shattered by the ferocity of the explosion.

Ker-ump! Ker-ump! Ker-ump! Crack!

Again the eruption of noise, worse if anything. In the

utter silence which followed, a hail of sand and mud and stone and shale rose like a fountain, its downfall tumbling in slow-motion. Despite their distance from it, light debris spattered their shoulders and heads and upraised hands.

Ker-ump! Ker-ump! Ker-ump! Crack!

The crowd about-turned to face the wall, wiser now, hunched up. Someone bulky leaned over Aideen and she liked the body's protection. Ben was sandwiched between two burly men, who were saying a number of words he had seen written on lavatory walls but never heard spoken aloud. He gritted his teeth waiting for the next explosion but the single 'All Clear' note of the siren blew. The rope barrier was removed and the crowd surged forward, laughing, talking, assuring each other they had not minded the explosion a whit, nor felt the least fear, nor cared about being showered by harbour floor debris.

'Huh!' said Ben. 'Do you hear them? They were just as scared as I was.'

'Liars,' Aideen said, plainly. '*I* never want to hear any more like that anyway. My ears are still ringing. Let's get our bikes and go home.'

'Always supposing they haven't been hammered to bits by all that stuff falling on them,' said Ben, 'but I think they should have been out of range.'

'We'd better check.' Aideen sprang off like a dynamo, clutching at her library books, the blue coolbag bouncing from its shoulder strap.

A few sandy pebbles scattered the ground around the station railings but the chained up bicycles were safe. Aideen hauled up the string beneath her T-shirt, which held the key for her bicycle lock.

'Hang on a tick,' said Ben, 'I'd like a quick peek to see if all that blasting has made any difference. We can't come tomorrow and they'll be on to something else by the day after, I bet.'

It made sense. Aideen dropped back the string and key.

'Just a quick look then,' she said, sure there would be little to see for the crowd was melting away. They stepped to the edge.

'It isn't any different from the last time. I just feel higher up.' She felt indignant. 'All that fuss and pother for nothing.'

Ben stared intently at the bedrock depths. The liquid mud bottom was the same revolting mess all right. A couple of figures in thigh boots plodded around, inspectors of some kind, he supposed. He narrowed his eyes, wishing for binoculars. The men did not look official somehow, no helmets for one thing ....

Aideen's sharp elbow roused him. 'Hey! Are you going to sleep, or what? Come on. We've looked.'

'All right, all right, I'm coming. I was just watching those two men down there. I wonder what they're doing.'

She gave a casual glance, then caught her breath. 'What are *they* doing there, both of them, and *together*?'

'Who do you mean?'

'Who do you think I mean? Mr Carrigan and Mr Kinseely, of course. Do you think anyone knows they're there, anyone official, I mean?'

'Are you sure it's them?'

'Of course it is. You know I can see miles further than

you. But what are they doing? Why are they there? That's what I'd like to know.'

'We won't find out from up here. Anyway, they seem to have gone behind something now. I can't see them at all.'

'There's nothing to go behind. That's funny. They were as clear as anything a second ago.' Aideen leaned over the pier edge precariously, searching the harbour's muddy floor. 'They've vanished. I hope they're OK.'

'Well, they can't drown, the water is only knee deep. Maybe they just walked off while we were talking.' He checked his watch. 'Aideen, guess what, it's 9.51 and ten seconds. We've exactly nine minutes to get home, never mind into bed.'

The uphill bicycle ride home broke Olympic records but they made the deadline, just. There had been several telephone calls from their friends. None could come tomorrow.

'I feel their families think we're a bit mad sometimes,' smiled Riona. 'Some people like to take their time about deciding things.'

Neither had the children any time to tell of the explosions, or the two half-brothers' mysterious appearance and disappearance in the harbour basin.

I still don't understand about them having different names, even if they have one different parent, thought Ben, in his bed. Something wrong about that somehow. He toppled over a great cliff of sleep. Climbing back to wakefulness was hard labour. He shook his head, bewildered by his mother's call. How could it be seven in the morning? He curled back into a knot under the duvet but his mother's firm hand still shook his shoulder.

'Isle of Man, remember?'

Recollection came. Ben sat with a jerk, wide awake, ready for action. 'Where's Aideen? Is she up?'

'Just about where you are, I imagine,' smiled Riona. 'Maddy's gone to wake her. Put a sweater on, it's pretty cool and a bit cloudy, I'm afraid. Breakfast's ready when you are.'

But they'd all slipped behind schedule somehow and now Maddy raced the Mini against the clock all along the new Bus Clearway. 'Keep every eye skinned for Guardians of the Law.' Her eyes gleamed mischief. But early morning traffic was light and not a Garda was in sight, except at the checkpoint entrance to the industrial highway leading to the docks. The car sped past timber yards, warehouses, gasometers and petrol refinery storage tanks to the car park at the ferry's jetty. They sprinted to the ticket office.

'The boat is bigger than I thought,' puffed Ben.

'You can't even read *Isle of Man Steamship Packet* now,' complained Aideen, 'the letters are too big when you're close up to it.'

'Go ahead, you two, and find us a sheltered place to sit. Near the funnel if you can.'

'Go on,' said Riona, handing over the boarding passes, 'we'll be there in a minute or two.'

As they had been amongst the last to board, the children could only find space enough for two on the wooden seating within the funnel's curving wall. Aideen tested it for their mothers' wind protection. Neither she nor Ben would need to sit.

'Nice fresh breeze.' Ben watched the wheeling gulls watching him.

'Uh, oh!' said Aideen.

'What's that for?'

'Guess where my sea sick pills are?'

'Oh no,' said Ben, 'you didn't ....'

'I did. They're at home.'

'Double Oh!' said Ben.

Aideen owned a stomach allergic to all bouncy motions. Even riding a seesaw could play havoc with it. She crossed her fingers and pulled a wry face.

'It's only a *light* breeze,' Ben amended his weather forecast.

'Don't say anything to Mum,' she hissed. 'Maybe I've grown out of it overnight.'

Maddy and Riona pushed picnic bags under the seats and examined their fellow passengers restlessly parading the decks.

'It reminds me a bit of ....' Maddy began, then stopped, looking at Aideen, her eyes softly sad.

Aideen stared into her mother's eyes, remembering that last package holiday to Greece with Dad, the island boat trips, being seasick. She had been six years of age. 'Oh, yes, I remember, Mum.' Aideen's smile became gentle. For a puzzling second she felt grown up.

'It's blowing more than I expected,' said Riona, 'but the sun's coming out. It's going to be a lovely trip.'

The engines rumbled into action. In seconds, they were moving downriver, passing docks choc-a-bloc with cargo ships from far-away countries, passing oil terminal storage tanks tinted grey, yellow, green, blue, leaving behind the twin scarlet and white skyscraper chimneys of the Pigeon House power station, cruising between the mile long arms of the Bull Wall and

Poolbeg, channelled through the guiding buoys and blinking lights into the open sea. The children held the *Lady of Man's* rails, watching every inch of rocky coast slip by.

'We're there, we're there. Look! There it is — Whisky Cove!' Ben shouted into Aideen's ear.

'Who are those people on the beach?' she shouted through the wind. 'They're waving something. Look, Ben.'

'It's our flag, it's Flag o' the Woods!'

'It's them. Oh, look, even Brains is there!'

The children jumped up and down as though on springs, screaming greetings to their friends, waving in a frenzy of excitement. Riona and Maddy came running. The deck passengers became infected, eager to share this bonus of gaiety. The deck itself quivered beneath their feet. Then, suddenly, unexpectedly, it shuddered.

'That's peculiar ....' Ben stopped, startled into silence by a resounding crack from the boat's stern, where the rudder churned the sea to froth. A second, sharper crack sounded, more alarming. Broken clumps of water somersaulted into the sea above the rudder like acrobatic jellyfish. The ship's engines stopped, speed slowed. Abreast of the lighthouse on the point, they hove to, wallowing in the choppy sea. Aideen's stomach heaved, too. The loud hailer system crackled.

> This is your Captain speaking. Due to circumstances beyond our control, we must return to dock in order to check damage sustained to the ship's rudder. It is regretted that the passage may not be quite as smooth as normal. Every effort will be made to obtain a reserve ship to facilitate residents from the Isle of Man. Day Trip

ticket holders will be refunded at the terminal. Please accept our regrets on this occasion.

'Just get back,' whispered Aideen, feeling green.

'Oh, oh!' Maddy knew the signs. She knew her daughter. 'Your travel pills. You've forgotten them, haven't you?' She scrabbled about in her bag. 'You always forget them. I might have some somewhere. Ah, ha! Here we are.' She slit the foil wrapping with her finger nail.

Aideen snatched the rescuing tablet. Act fast, act fast! She urged it to dissolve, gluing her eyes to nearby objects which remained *still*, waiting for the medication to control the nausea.

Ben spared her a side-glance from the corner of his eye. 'OK yet?' He was preoccupied by pinpointing every landmark on Oisín's coastline, and studying the skilful manoeuvres the Captain used to nurse his craft back to port without any further damage.

Aideen nodded and drank the glass of soda-water Riona brought back to her from the saloon bar.

'Mm. Thanks, Auntie. I'm OK now, I ... I think.'

Riona had also brought a Bacardi and coke for herself and Maddy, and a 7-Up for Ben. 'I asked one of the crew if he knew what had damaged the fins, or whatever they're called,' she said.

'Rudders, Mum,' said Ben.

'Rudders, then. Anyway, he said it sounded to him like a stone being fired at them from a huge catapult, only you don't get anyone using catapults under the water. He was being funny, I suppose.'

'They have to say something,' said Maddy.

'A catapult?' Ben understood what the man meant. It had sounded like that sort of crack. He sipped at his 7-Up, swaying his body in tune to the heaving *Lady of Man*. A certain odour tickled his nostrils. Yuk! Stewards began giving travel sickness bags to some passengers in need of them but Aideen was not one of them. The tablet seemed to be working.

'There's Far Hills cottage,' she yelled. 'Can you see it, Mum? *There*. Look for the clump of trees.' Nearby passengers began searching for it, too, lit by her delight. 'And that's Mr Carrigan's cottage. See? Right up on the Hill. It's so white in the sun I can hardly look. D'ye see it, Ben?'

Ben shielded his eyes. 'Well, I'm nearly blinded, so I'm not sure. I suppose it's his windows flashing the light back, like a mirror does when you're trying to dazzle someone.' Then his brain clicked. 'It's his telescope, that's what it is. I'll bet he's been watching us.'

'He's probably seen whatever made those cracks,' she said. 'Let's go and ask him as soon as we get home. Then we could tell the shipping people ....'

'No, we couldn't,' Ben was firm. 'We promised Mr Carrigan to keep quiet about his sparetime activities, remember.'

'Oh, yes, I forgot, but he could tell *us*.'

'He could, I suppose, if he knows.'

'But will he tell?' said Maddy, later, as she whirled the Mini into Far Hill's hedge-hidden entrance, ignoring the panicky horn blow from the car following.

'Whether he will or whether he won't,' said Riona, 'we'd better either have a second breakfast now, or an early lunch, and it's bacon and eggs either way.'

'Brunch, in fact,' said Maddy. 'Goody.'

'In that delightful cottage we admired from the ocean wave, you mean?' grinned Aideen.

'That's the one,' said her mother, 'and then you can hop on to Mr Carrigan's bus, or trot up to his house if he's off duty, and see what's what.'

'Flag o' the Woods first,' said Ben. 'I'll bet the others are there waiting for us by this time. Let's go, Aideen. They'll be dying to know why the boat had to turn back.' He chewed the last of his toast.

So is Mac Alúishin dying to know, thought Aideen, running across the field. He feels closer than ever. She could see the other children churning about at the edge of Flag o' the Woods, obviously Mac Alúishin injected and agog with news of their own, and no one heard anyone else in the babbling chorus when they met.

'Stop!' ordered Ben. 'Nuala, you tell whatever it is, then Aideen can tell about us.'

Nuala closed her eyelids a long moment, then spoke. 'He was there again, that man, madder than ever. *Furious* he was, galloping the poor horse like a lunatic. You'd think no horse could gallop up and over those craggy steps to Roshín Rock, wouldn't you? Well, *he* did poor thing, and that madman rider shouting at us and waving an enormous catapult ....'

'A what?' Ben gasped. He looked at Aideen, wide-eyed, shaken.

'Don't be silly,' she said.

'But you know,' Nuala did another eyelids close-open, 'he didn't come back again like last time and, apart from swimming the horse around to Strand Road, there's no other way he could go, is there? Did you ever see anyone riding a horse and waving a huge catapult? He's mad, I tell you.'

'Was he *using* the catapult?' Ben's mind teased him.

'On a galloping horse?' exclaimed Micky. 'Are you as crazy as him?'

'It's your turn to tell, Aideen,' Brains butted in. 'Was it good on the *Lady of Man*? I still think Dad's mean not letting me go, just because we're going to Crete next month ... it's not one bit fair ....'

'If you stop moaning a minute, I'll tell you,' said Aideen. She did, forgetting neither her queasy stomach, Mr Carrigan's glinting telescope nor the crewman's joke about a catapult.

'Oh, I get what you mean, now, Ben,' said Micky, 'but it couldn't be done you know, it's too far from land, and the crack noise came from underneath, you said.'

'I believe he'd be mad enough to *try* anything, that man,' said Nuala, 'but I agree, it would be impossible.'

'There are more things in Heaven and earth, Horatio ....'

'Oh, do shut up, Brains,' Micky stopped Brains short. 'You did that one on us yesterday.'

'You didn't say if you'd seen the seals, Aideen,' said Ferna. 'They must've ducked under the minute the boat passed because they'd gone afterwards.'

'Did *you* see any seals, Ben?' Aideen asked him.

'No, I didn't,' he said. 'Sensible, aren't they, getting out of the way? I bet they hate boat engines churning up the water.'

Aideen screwed her face up. 'You don't think,' she said, dismayed, 'that Button went too near to one and got hurt that way?'

'Could be,' Micky said. 'Getting swirled about, he might have been flung against one of the blades. Rotten thing that boat.' He sounded quite savage.

'Maybe that's why Mr Kinseely went crackers yesterday,' Ben nodded.

'Who,' asked Nuala, 'is Mr Kinseely?'

'Gosh, Ben, I forgot they didn't know about us meeting him.' Aideen began the story. 'It was after you'd gone yesterday ....'

When she reported Mr Kinseely's scorn for Micky's snorkel and flippers the boy waxed indignant but, at the same time, was anxious to learn about their new swimming skills.

'We'll teach you,' Ben said. He felt smug.

'All of you,' added Aideen, '*after* we've asked Mr Carrigan if he saw anything through his telescope. I'm off to stop the bus and find out.'

9

Sea Foam and Starshine

'Off duty, he is,' shouted Paddy Joe over the engine roar. 'Hop on. I'll drop all of ye at the foot of his lane.' He excused himself for giving them a free ride. 'Sure, it's only a couple o' stops up the road.'

'Thanks, Paddy Joe,' they yelled.

'Don't be telling anyone else now.' Paddy Joe revved away with a nod and a wink.

They felt a Mac Alúishin transfusion zip them vigorously up the steep laneway, taking its hairpin-hook turn into the East Mountain foothills towards Look-Out Cottage, the lane growing narrower and more potholed by the foot. Aideen, in the lead as usual, rounded the last bend. She stopped dead.

'You'll never guess,' she said, 'not in a hundred years.' She moved to one side.

'It's *that man's* horse,' whispered Nuala, appalled.

The creamy stallion stood quietly beside an ivy-wrapped tree trunk, swishing the summer flies into the air with a plumy tail of silvery hairs. Folds of soft green material lay draped across his back. Gently, he scratched his chin on the rough surface of Mr Carrigan's garden wall.

'He *is* beautiful,' sighed Ferna.

'*Why* is he there? That's what I'd like to know.' Micky paused. 'You don't think that fella's inside, do you ...?'

'If he is, I'm going home,' said Brains.

But Aideen trusted Mr Carrigan. 'Don't be silly,' she said. 'If the horse is here, then it must be for a good reason. Maybe he's pulled a muscle or something, galloping about the cliff path like that, and Mr Carrigan's doctoring him. Well, he might be. Anyway, I'm going to see if he's there, Mr Carrigan, I mean. Come on, Ben. The rest of you wait here.'

'I'll wait,' Ferna agreed. 'The horse seems gentle enough now. I'd give anything to ride him, really.'

Reassured, the others sat down on the bank beside her. Didn't she know a good lot about horses after all? Ben and Aideen walked forward, their rubber flipflops soundless in the dust of the lane. The horse widened its white velvety nostrils into a friendly 'Puff!' when they opened the gate, but took no further notice.

'I'm glad about that,' whispered Ben, relaxing.

'Mm. I felt a bit wobbly,' Aideen admitted. She tapped the brass dolphin doorknocker and then reared back in fright at its instant opening.

'Ah, there you are,' said Mr Carrigan. 'I thought you might be along one of these minutes. We've been waiting for you, you might say.'

We? Ben darted a glance at Aideen. He saw her nervous swallowing. So did Mr Carrigan.

'Ah, sure, 'tis only Mr Kinseely and myself, and you

know *him* well enough now, don't you?' His grin was crooked. 'What about the rest of them? Will they be waiting out there for you?' He handed Ben a large packet of Liquorice Allsorts. 'Run back there with these, should keep everyone happy for a spell.' He and Aideen watched Ben edge past the white horse. 'I always liked Liquorice Allsorts myself,' he confided to her.

'That's a lovely horse,' she hinted.

'Sea Foam is a beautiful creature, no more and no less,' he agreed, in an edgy tone of voice. 'He's been misused entirely these last few days. Such hard going is no use to the likes of him, I tell you. He's used to better.' His eyes glittered blue sparks. 'He won't do it again, I'll tell you that as well, the mad eejit.'

'You mean Sea Foam is a mad eejit?' she asked, entranced by the name.

'I mean the horse *rider*,' his voice had a dark tone.

'I'm glad you're stopping him, then,' said Aideen. 'He really scared us the other day, and this morning ....'

'I know about this morning.'

'Nuala thinks we ought to tell the police about him ....'

Mr Carrigan laughed. 'The police, how are ye, they're no use at all in such a matter, my girl. I'm the boyo to fix it, and fix it I will, don't worry. Ah, Ben, there you are, you're back. That's the ticket. Now, come on in, the two of you, or my darling brother will be dozing off on us.'

Ben listened to Aideen's rapidly whispered retelling of Mr Carrigan's remarks as they followed him to the room where they had watched the film, but Mr Kinseely was not asleep. He reclined against a fat cushion of glistening brown seaweed piled high on the table (just like the nest Button had in the home movie), and he was wearing an ancient towelling bathrobe, frayed and jagged at collar, sleeve and hem. 'Ye didn't go far on that Isle of Man yoke after all,' he greeted them, with a triumphant flash of beautiful teeth.

'That's enough of that, Lir,' said Mr Carrigan. 'Get off that table and act respectable. What'll these two be thinkin' of you at all?'

'Ah, sure, ye know I'm only teasing, don't ye?' Mr Kinseely swung down from the table to a chair, still smiling.

Ben told both men about the *Lady of Man's* morning mishap and how they had seen the sun glinting on the lens of the telescope in Look-Out Cottage.

'We *thought* that's what it might be,' added Aideen, more tactfully.

'Then we wondered if you'd been looking, Mr Carrigan, because no one on the boat knew what caused the damage, not even the Captain, and it would be nice to know ....' Ben stopped.

'Oh, *he* knows all right. Me big brother knows a lot of things, spying with that telescope there.' Lir looked at his elder brother with no pleasure.

'Spying is not a very nice word to be using, so it's not, Lir,' Mr Carrigan said. 'I'm only keeping me eye on things, as well you know.' His tufty eyebrows wriggled. 'It's not called Look-Out Cottage for no reason, after all.'

'No, I suppose not,' said Ben, 'but *did* you see anything happen out there this morning?'

Aideen had a sudden flashback. 'And was it you two down in the harbour after those explosions last night?'

'Hold your horses now, Lir,' Mr Carrigan said,

touching his brother's shoulder for a second. 'I'll be telling them, not you.' He turned to the children again. 'There's a lot else you have to know before we can enlarge on that. It's not going to be easy for you, I know that well, but we've decided it's you and Ben we'll trust ... we thought it would have been the other two, but there you are.' He sighed heavily, inconclusively.

'The other two?' Ben said.

'He means Declan and Fintan,' said Lir Kinseely.

A weight pressed down on Aideen's shoulders. She had not once thought of the Terrible Twins since sighting the Russian Button on Button's flipper. She had been wrapped in her own enjoyment. Ben saw the tears film over her green eyes and knew that she, too, felt his own sudden cloud of guilt. How could he have forgotten, even for a minute?

'Ah, sure, you have to go on living, you know,' said Mr Carrigan, reading their stricken faces. 'Isn't that the way life is arranged for us, and isn't it just as well? Wouldn't we go right out of our minds grieving twenty-four hours of the day? You've not forgotten your friends, and you won't ever, not really. They'll be in your hearts the length of your own lives.'

'Thanks, Mr Carrigan.' Ben felt his chest loosen and lighten. Mr Carrigan can fix people as well as seals and horses, he thought, turning to Aideen in relief.

She was still pondering Mr Carrigan's words, memorising them, but her face had settled down. 'I don't know how you knew what I was thinking, Mr Carrigan, but you did. I think it's their not being found that's worst of all.'

'The Oisín born never return,' muttered Mr Kinseely,

grinding his teeth a little.

'Is that really true?' asked Ben. 'Because it's a very queer thing if it is. I mean, what difference does it make? The sea doesn't care where people come from surely?'

'No, the *sea* doesn't care.' Mr Kinseely shook his head, taking a sidelong look at his brother.

'I mean,' Ben was determined to be logical, 'are there any records to prove it?'

'You mean a lot of names and dates written on a bit of paper?' asked Mr Carrigan. 'Well, nothing of that sort exactly but, just the same, there's been a queer few, down all the years. Did you never read the notice board outside the Lifeboat House down there at the pier end?'

'Once or twice, we did.' Aideen was puzzled.

'Well, just you check that shipwreck and rescue log with old newspaper reports, and you can get to read them in the newspaper offices, if you ask nicely. You'll see that anybody not rescued, or washed ashore, turns out to be Oisín born.'

'True,' said his brother.

'Mind you,' continued Mr Carrigan, 'there's no newspapers much to be seen before the year 1800 or so.'

'I'd like to do a project using those records, Aideen,' Ben said.

'Maybe we could,' she said, smiling.

'Before you start one of them project things,' said Mr Kinseely, 'what about that telescope gazin' ye've got on for tonight?' He winked at his brother.

'*Tonight*. Wow!' said Ben.

'What time? Can everyone come?' Aideen's breathing hurried.

'No!' Their friends eating Liquorice Allsorts out there

must know nothing. '*No one,*' repeated Mr Carrigan in this new, remarkably firm voice, 'is to know you're coming, except your Mammies, o'course, or everything could be spoiled entirely.' His eyebrows quirked. 'You promise now. Cross your hearts and hope to die?'

They did so, thus making Mr Carrigan's secrets untellable, proud to be the only two people he could trust.

'Remember the Third Monkey!' Ben chuckled under his breath.

Lir looked anxious. 'Will your Mammies let ye out so late in the night?'

Aideen was all innocence. 'We told them about Mr Carrigan watching the stars and ....'

'And they both said we'd be mad not to grab at the chance.' Ben's grin swept them like a lighthouse beam.

The brothers exchanged satisfied glances. 'Rocks o'sense, those two girls,' Mr Carrigan said. He would call to Far Hills Cottage for them at eleven thirty sharp and see that they were back home an hour later. It might be cold outdoors so they had better dress warmly.

'What about Sea Foam?' Aideen asked, daring to pat the horse's silken nose as the brothers escorted them to the gateway.

'Ah, that beauty will be safe home in his proper surroundings this nightfall,' Mr Carrigan assured her.

~

The afternoon in Whisky Cove dragged like a heavy anchor. Keeping Look-Out Cottage secrets from their friends, whilst dying to tell them everything, took a deal of doing and drained Ben and Aideen to the point of exhaustion. So, after the evening meal, when their mothers sent them to rest in bed with a book, they drowsed more than read through the waiting hours. Just before the deadline, they put on the cord jeans, thick socks, wellie-boots, Aran sweaters and anoraks Riona had assembled, while Maddy strengthened their insides with scalding hot Bovril and baked-in-their-jackets potatoes. Mr Carrigan's horn sounded at eleven thirty to the second.

He was alone. 'Lir never rides in a car if he can help it,' chuckled Mr Carrigan. 'Sure, my brother's hardly civilised at all a lot of the time.' The dashboard light lit his smiling, higgledy-piggledy teeth. 'But, there, wasn't he always the mischievous one?' Mischievous, thought Ben, yes, that's the right word. 'Anyway,' Mr Carrigan concluded, 'he'll be there by now and waiting.'

The night glowed clear. Scudding clouds raced across the full moon's bright face. Outside Look-Out Cottage, on the small terrace facing seaward, the telescope stood ready on its tripod. Mr Kinseely was absorbed, adjusting it finely.

'There now,' he greeted them, his teeth gleaming like mother-of-pearl in the starlight. His greeting turned into a farewell. 'I'll be off to me job now,' he said.

'Job? What job?' Ben asked in surprise. It seemed a funny time to start work.

'Well, it's sort of about the harbour ceiling,' began Mr Kinseely.

'Floor,' said his brother.

'It *was* you two down there last night, wasn't it?' interrupted Aideen.

'They think they're doing great things with their dry docks and deep anchorage,' said Mr Carrigan, without a yea or a nay to Aideen's remark, 'and some of that will be good for the fishermen right enough, but they don't know how much damage that blasting is doing elsewhere, now do they?'

'Too deep altogether, too deep,' intoned Lir Kinseely.

'And yesterday evening's blasting seriously upset things for them, us, I mean. Something's got to be done before there's a complete disaster. The nerves of the both of us are all of a quiver with it all, wondering what to be doing to put a stop to it. It's not easy keeping Lir here from going mad sometimes. Yes,' repeated Mr Carrigan, seeing Lir's scowl, 'and I'm going to put a stop to that, too. Once we get it all worked out, he'll be going back to sea for good and all. Best place for him.'

Lir nodded. 'Never mind that. Just let them see what they're to see, a thing or three, and keep to the arrangements.' He grinned impishly, then whistled sharply through puckered lips, whereupon Sea Foam stepped into view around the corner of the cottage, his coat a fluorescent white in the stars' shine. Aideen drew breath at the horse's beauty. In one subtle movement, Lir sat astride the animal, snatching the length of green cloth draping its withers, whirling it round his own shoulders, whence it floated as he cajoled Sea Foam into a pirouette. They took the wall in one dangerous leap. 'Keep watching, brother!' his voice called above the clatter of swift hooves.

'We'll do that all right,' muttered Mr Carrigan, fixing his eye to the telescope's eye piece. 'Orion, where are you? Ah, there you are.' He held it steady for Ben. 'Orion, the Hunter, constellation, at your service, sir,' he said.

'I thought you said Sea Foam would be back home tonight,' Aideen accused him.

'Ah, sure, isn't he heading there this very minute?' replied Mr Carrigan, urging Ben to yield the eyepiece to Aideen.

'You mean that's the last time we'll ever see him?' Ben's interests became divided abruptly. 'Where's the Plough constellation, Mr Carrigan?'

'Near enough, it is.' Mr Carrigan divided his answers. 'Well, maybe one more bit of a glimpse before the night's out.' He bent down and refocused. 'Now there's the Plough for you — the Big Dipper they call it in the US of A.'

'That sort of soup-ladle shape, you mean?' asked Aideen.

'Mm ... but the Great Bear it's known as in most places. Now isn't that the grand name? Ursa Major it is in the Latin language, at least that's what young Brains said a few months since.'

'He would!' Ben snorted. 'But isn't the Plough supposed to point to the North Star? You always have to know where that is, in case you get lost.'

I don't, thought Aideen, knowing she wasn't able to work out any compass points whatever, ever, not even in her home surroundings — she would have to stay lost until a search party came to the rescue.

Just then Mr Carrigan asked Ben to use the light switch of his watch for a time check. 'Ten to twelve already!' He swivelled the telescope to the glow of lights outlining Oisín and its harbour between the hills. 'Quiet now,' he said, 'it's time to be watching after Lir.' He stood rigid, statuelike.

'Mr Kinseely's up to something,' whispered Ben.

Aideen could not say why but a sudden apprehension seized her.

'Ha!' said Mr Carrigan. 'Take a look through this, one of ye, and tell me whatever it is ye see — me eyes are blurry with watching so close.'

He was right. It was close all right. Aideen could see the floodlit sea-wall bounding the harbour as if it was yards away instead of a mile or more. And riding nonchantly along the Pier's top level was Mr Kinseely! She could not make out what it was that was causing two lolloping shadows trailing the ground behind him.

'Ha,' said Mr Carrigan again, hearing Aideen's report. 'That's the ticket. Did he give any bit of a wave at all?'

Eagerly, Ben snatched at his turn to investigate. 'They're not shadows, Aideen, they look more like ....' He stopped short then. 'Mr Kinseely's waving now, Mr Carrigan, he's waving like fury.'

'Time to go, so.' Mr Carrigan rammed on his tram driver cap and jog-trotted to the Mini van. 'Hurry now,' he called to them.

'But the telescope ...?' Aideen said in dismay.

Indignation filled Ben. 'Surely we're not going home *already*?'

'Get in. Get in,' said Mr Carrigan, tetchy now. 'Hasn't Lir been fixing for us to see what's what? Weren't you listening at all last evening? Isn't it your help we're needing and aren't you the two we're trusting to do it?' He stopped talking as the van jerked over the lane's bumps. 'I know, I know,' he said, then, somewhat sheepishly, aware of their taken-aback faces. 'Are ye worrying what your Mammies might think, dashing off this way?' They nodded. 'It'll be no harm at all, no harm at all,' he reassured them, 'sure they'd be dying to give a hand themselves.' He changed gear for the steep run down the Hill. 'Ah, sure, not one lie did I tell either. Didn't we look at the stars like I promised?'

Put that way they had to agree, but all the same ....

Mr Carrigan switched off the main light-beam and glanced keenly left and right as soon as they reached the harbour road. It was deserted. He sighed in relief, slipping the van quietly into the shadow cast by an upturned boat on the slipway. In the moonlight, the harbour floor's excavated hillocks and hollows and silent machinery resembled an abandoned space exploration project. The children edged closer, looking into the floodlit harbour basin. It proved positively cheerful, if still ugly, more of the here and now about it. Mr Carrigan double-checked that no Garda paced his beat, nor solitary late night walker exercised his dog, before he stepped onto the rough, rock-strewn causeway behind the gaggle of notice boards forbidding everything. He smiled crookedly. 'Do you trust me now, or don't ye?'

Relying utterly on instinct, they nodded.

'Then just follow my footsteps,' he said, fitting his own feet into a trail of existing imprints. Long shadows forged ahead of their bodies in the harsh neon glare. A ladder-top etched itself in stark black outlines on the left. 'Ha!' said Mr Carrigan, 'good lad himself. He's fixed things all right. Down we go now.' He grasped the ladder's side rails to begin the long climb downwards.

Aideen sucked in her breath.

'Don't look,' said Ben. 'Pretend it's a ship's ladder. Go down backwards and you won't even notice.'

'That's the ticket,' said Mr Carrigan, seeing Aideen's confidence increase rung by rung.

Having a head for heights, Ben enjoyed a ladder as springy as a diving board himself but forbore saying so for Aideen's sake. He stepped off the bottom rung onto a sort of concrete staging-post, where began a further vertical descent via iron rungs cemented into the sheer wall facade, cascading ceaselessly to the mudcovered, slimy regions far below. That demanded an utter concentration of nerve and sinew from all three of them. Ben valiantly tried to joke himself out of a severe attack of after-tremble. *Terra firma*, at last, as Brains would say, only it's not very firm, he told himself.

'Lean against the wall, lad.' He heard Mr Carrigan's voice. 'Sure, aren't we all shaking like leaves, so we'll shut our eyes and stay quiet a minute and have a couple o' breaths for ourselves.'

'That's a great place for sleeping, I don't think!' Lir Kinseely's penetrating whisper whisked their eyes open and stemmed their trembles.

'Ah, there you are, Lir.' Mr Carrigan accepted his brother's come-and-go habits calmly but the children were nonplussed. There had been neither sight nor sound of him seconds ago. How on earth ...?

'Of course, here I am. Ages I've been waiting — ye know the tide's only right betweentimes.'

'I know, I know,' soothed Mr Carrigan, 'but it's the time we agreed on. You just think it's longer since you've been waiting about a bit. And we were only restin' our nerves a little after steeplejacking down.'

Lir's beautiful smile shone out in the arc-light's glare. 'Ah, don't be minding me. Ye're only human, isn't that right? What with one thing and another, I've gone a bit cranky tonight. I should be at home resting meself.'

'You'll be there soon enough and for as long as you like,' said Mr Carrigan, 'then you'll be as happy as Larry.' He gave the overlooking landscape a quick once-over. All clear. 'Stop talking now and get going.'

With one hand, Mr Kinseely grabbed Aideen's and with the other snatched up a muddy plank lying at his feet, kicking another towards Mr Carrigan and Ben.

'Where's Sea Foam?' Aideen wanted to know.

'Waiting for me below, of course, where else?' said Mr Kinseely.

Aideen eyed the shining wastes of mud, murky pools and constructed slipways and runways that lay ahead with apprehension. Her rubber boots were being sucked off her feet by the mud but Mr Kinseely strode lightly onwards wearing no boots at all. Ben noticed Mr Carrigan's bare feet. That's the secret of success, he thought, and bent down to remove his own boots.

'Not for you two, no,' said Mr Carrigan.

Mr Kinseely threw his plank alongside a deep crack in the mud. 'You can start looking here,' he said.

At what were they to look? Ben asked, idly wondering why no water filled the cleft. Aideen sank to her hunkers on the plank and peered into the jagged gap. 'Is it what you call a fissure?' She knew the ground cracked open in hot countries and that earth tremors made even bigger clefts. Lir made no comment. He lifted the plank and marched towards the epicentre of last night's blasting, beckoning them across the numerous other rifts criss-crossing the bleak terrain. He halted beside an opening the width of a man's body. 'This one,' he announced, '*is* a fissure.' He slid his own and Mr Carrigan's planks across the menacing chasm, making a bridge upon which the brothers laid themselves prone from opposite ends, their heads meeting midway but levered sideways in order to gaze fixedly down the opening.

The children regarded one another with foreboding, no words needed. Their turn came next.

10

The Floor is the Ceiling

Ben expected a smothering, Stygian darkness, and dreaded it, whereas Aideen's mind writhed full of monster conger eels, but a gentle light dappled their eyelids, and curiosity opened them. It was like peering into a gigantic kaleidoscope, except that swift grey shapes wriggled across the tube's end instead of ever-changing colour patterns. It reminded Ben of the day he had examined a slide of amoeba under a microscope.

'Sea water makes that light this time o' night,' Mr Carrigan explained. 'They call it phosphorescence.'

Aideen had heard of that. 'It's weird, magicky, sort of,' she whispered. 'Is it very deep down there? The water, I mean.' The depth of the fissure was very obvious.

'There's what you might call a layer of water at the bottom,' Mr Carrigan said.

'Not deep enough,' Mr Kinseely growled, frowning.

'It looks as if the water is flowing,' said Ben. 'Is it? And what are all those shadowy things moving about?'

'No time for all that now. Tide's changing.' Lir jerked

at Aideen's leg. 'Come on. Stand up now. I've got to be going.'

As soon as they had gingerly inched off the planks Mr Kinseely bounced back on, swung onto his stomach and lowered himself into the chasm until only the pressure of his chin and ten finger tips upon the plank supported him.

Aideen stood statue-still, shocked. 'You're not going down *there*?'

'He'll kill himself,' Ben said, aghast.

Mr Carrigan remained calm. 'Not him. Don't you be worrying about him at all. There's ways and means, you know, and Lir has every one of them off by heart. Anyway, we have to be off.'

'*Off*? How do you mean, "be off"? You're not going to leave him?' No one, thought Ben, could do such a thing to their own half-brother.

Aideen said nothing, hypnotised by Lir Kinseely's mud-spattered but flashing smile.

'Off ye go,' said that man. 'Ye've a lot more to see this night. The boat's waiting there for ye.'

Boat? Aideen's bewilderment increased. What now? She watched his fingertips flicker upwards, let go. Her heart beat in unfamiliar, slow thumps.

'He's gone.' Ben's face felt drained of blood.

A faint, far away splash echoed. Mr Carrigan nodded. 'He's gone. There now. God bless him. No more talking now. There's the boat to be got hold of yet.'

Each step through the cloying mud, back to the precipice-like wall, and the terrifying climb up it, took every ounce of their strength. This must be how people feel when they lie down to die in Arctic snows rather than carry on, thought Aideen. Ben gritted his teeth against the pain of his knee and doggedly followed Mr Carrigan's tracks to the causeway's deepwater side, where moonlight took over from the arc lights, and yachts rocked in the shining water, masts and spars black lines against the sky. An old wooden rowing boat nudged its prow against the docked dredging platform. They stepped into the boat, still wondering where they were going. Mr Carrigan slipped a canoe paddle out from under his seat. 'Just what I need,' he muttered, pushed off with it, and finned the boat away. When he reached the shelter of two yachts anchored midway to the small lighthouse at the end of the pier, just out of range of its flickering beam, he slid the anchor into the water without a sound, without a ripple. 'Here's the spot,' he said, a strange note in his voice.

Their eyes dilated. What spot? The spot for what? Doubts swarmed about in their minds like wasps. He couldn't be going to ...? No. No! It was only in newspapers and on television that a family friend suddenly kidnapped or murdered neighbourhood children. Aideen's teeth bit and held on to a large chunk of inside lip. She watched Ben's lips twist into ever odder shapes.

'The two o' ye are looking all stiff,' Mr Carrigan whispered. His jutting eyebrows cast a shadow as far as his cheekbones. He withdrew the paddle from the water and took a penknife from his pocket. 'Ah, sure 'tis a bit cold,' he said. He poked about below his seat. 'Ah, ha!' A thermos flask in his hand. 'Here's the coffee.'

Coffee never tasted better, each hot sip melting away the children's fearfilled thoughts and tensions. The moonlight seeped colour from their faces still but

Aideen no longer felt pale. She was ready for anything and smiled easily at Mr Carrigan.

'Now then,' he said, 'the rest is simple enough.' He bent forward, and traced the penknife's blade around the outlines of several dark, wood-knot whorls set into the boat's smooth and varnished bottom, levering the pieces up into his hands. The children held the gunwales, waiting for the water to rush in. Was Mr Carrigan mad after all?

'We'll not sink at all, don't ye fear. Isn't there glass let into the holes?' said Mr Carrigan, as if that was the natural way for boat holes to be. 'Lie down on the bottom there and each o' ye put an eye to one o' the holes.'

They did so without a quibble, past astonishment. One look convinced Ben that he was heading straight for what his friends at school called the Funny House. He jerked away, shaken. He saw Aideen curving backwards from the waist, stock still, staring at him in fear. Mr Carrigan sat astride the centre seat, very alert.

'Is it frightened ye are? Ah, there now, there now.' He patted their heads as soothingly as he had the head of the seal he had operated on.

'I ... I ....' Aideen failed to work her tongue.

'It's true, it's true,' Mr Carrigan said.

'But ... it's ....'

'It is indeed. Indeed it is,' he agreed, sighing a little.

Ben nerved himself. 'I saw Oisín down there.' He kept his voice very flat.

'But it's up *there*.' Aideen waved a hand at the village silhouetted on the Hill behind them. 'Is it a sort of reflection?' Her own ears caught the shiver in her voice.

'Sure, aren't you the bright one entirely?' An enquiring expression sat on Mr Carrigan's face. 'Dare ye look any more?' he asked.

Ben dared, did, and the right word filtered into his mind. Replica. Yes. *An Oisín replica.* A sort of photocopy of Oisín, in fact, and yet .... It must be the combination of moonlight on the water, mixed up with the arc lights, that floated a mirror image below the boat somehow. That's what it must be. Like ... like ... well, like the way a camera film develops in some sort of chemical mixture. Something like that anyway. His head began to be muzzy from this midnight conjecturing. His squirms had churned up the water, distorting the scene, bringing uneven movement to it as well as an air of unreality.

Aideen's elbow checked him. 'Stay still,' she hissed, her imagination afire. Suddenly, vividly, a sentence in a book she had read at her grandmother's house one rainy day reprinted itself in her mind. '*Whatever's on the land, there's the same in the sea.*' In that book an old, old woman on the wild west coast of Ireland told strange tales around turf fires on winter nights. She told of a village on the sea-bed which she had seen whilst rowing herself home on a moonlit night.

Gossiping women stood in their cottage doorways down there, the old woman said, toddlers tugging at their ground-hugging skirts. Victorian ladies sauntered down the street holding parasols, others wore bustles and poke bonnets; one or two crinolined ladies strolled with grace, chatting with friends clad in the clothes of today. The times seemed to be all mixed up, the old woman said. Many of the men wore sailors' hats, ships' names written in gold on the circling rims, and their bell-bottom trousers flapped as they walked; others clumped along in seamen's boots, thick Aran sweaters, yellow oilskins and ripped-apart life jackets; young men and boys headed towards the sea in sandals and swimming costumes, towels in their hands; some of the men wore old-fashioned flat caps and country-thick suits. Children of all sizes and ages played together in a similar mix of clothes. They bowled hoops, whipped tops, batted battledores, rotated yo-yos, played Blind-man's Buff, hopscotch, tennis, hurley and cricket, threw skittles, bowls and balls left, right and centre. Each man, woman and child sparkled with so much liveliness and delight, the old woman said, that she wished she had been there herself.

That old woman's tale-telling had stuck in Aideen's mind and mixed itself up with the legend of the Children of Lir, those sad children who had been changed into swans compelled to wander lonely lakes and seas for 900 years. Aideen whispered as much of this as she could to Ben as they waited for the water to resettle into a steadier reflection. The old woman's story made sense of the disconcerting, double-vision version below them, this Oisín familiar, yet unfamiliar. *'Whatever's on the land, there's the same in the sea.'*

Whirling thoughts all but overcame them. The phosphorescent glow they had first seen at the bottom of Mr Kinseely's fissure shone overall, casting neither shade nor shadow on the village Ben instantly named Oisín-Below-the-Water. The quivering replica fascinated them, called to them. At the sea end of the underwater village, where the pier began, what looked like a rubber cat-door flap (but horse-sized) was set into the sea-wall (which was *not* so in the sea-wall of Oisín above them).

Through that black rubber flap, supple, rounded objects pushed now and then, rolling forward into a somersault which, at its conclusion, showed the object to be human, either a boy, girl or an adult springing agilely erect. Occasionally, an undersea villager pushed the cat-door outwards in a head first diving action, heels in the air, and disappeared. The ground all around the cat-door shone wet. Finally, the flap strained into an enormous bulge as a large creamy body charged through in a reckless plunge, rolling forward like a ball of candyfloss to spring up airily, horse high. *Sea Foam.* On his back Lir Kinseely. A tremendous surge of Mac Alúishin effervescence raced through the children.

'*He* is Mac Alúishin!' Aideen felt faint, revelation flooding her.

That truth hit Ben at the same instant. '*He* is the mad rider!' he gasped.

The water stilled. The Oisín-Below-the-Water assumed 3-D clarity. The children froze. Lir Kinseely, Mac Alúishin, the mad rider — all three of him — stared up into their eyes, his own as iridescent as opals, his hair whorled and shining like a golden cap; his wide smile, pure mother-of-pearl, radiated warmth to the inner core of them. He bowed, then pointed behind him to two smaller bodies thrusting through the cat-door, uncurling in a single, smooth bounce. Two boys. Fintan ... Declan!

The two tilted their heads, looked straight at Ben and Aideen and grinned broadly, making cheerful, thumbs-up signals, jiggling about as exuberantly as ever did the Terrible Twins. Slowly then, with great deliberation,

Fintan swung to and fro something suspended from his index finger. A catapult. He mimed a load-and-fire manoeuvre, aiming vertically upwards, his face alight with mischief. Ben sucked in his breath, astounded, reading the message clearly. Declan opened flat the palm of his hand beneath their gaze. They watched Fintan pluck the *Russian Button* from it, load and fire, straight at them.

The water shattered.

~

'Ah, don't be going to sleep on me now. It's late it's getting.'

The children looked at Mr Carrigan in amazement. Their boat was moored alongside the slipway where the Mini van was parked.

'There now, that's the ticket,' said Mr Carrigan. 'I can't be having you late home to your Mammies, now can I?'

Their minds moved as sluggishly as their limbs. A slow-motion, drugged feeling of lassitude enveloped them. Drugged? The word beat back and forth in Aideen's head like a pendulum. The coffee? That possibility simmered to the surface in reply. She turned to examine Mr Carrigan closely as soon as they were in the van.

He met her gaze. 'Tomorrow,' he said softly, in answer, switching on the engine. 'Now you're tired to pieces. Just tired, that's all.'

He had to beep his horn for Maddy and Riona to come and help the children indoors and into bed. So great was their exhaustion, every thought instantaneously ceased.

11

Underwater Ways

Ben flicked open the curtain to check his watch readout. The sun was blazing so it did not mean twelve midnight. 'Aideen,' he yelled at the top of his voice, 'it's tomorrow!'

She shoved open his door. 'I know it is. Stop shouting. Mum says Mr Carrigan's coming down after lunch, and he'd be much obliged if we said nothing about anything until then, and she also said, as she doesn't know what he's on about, maybe we'd better do as he says for now. She doesn't look all that pleased. Neither of them do,' Aideen ended.

'You've got huge black blobs under both your eyes,' Ben said.

'So have you. Aunt Riona says it's exhaustion.'

'Oh.' Ben paused. 'What d'ye think, Aideen? I mean, we did see what we saw, or did we?'

She was cautious. In today's sunlight, last night held the characteristics of a dream. '*Then* we did. I *thought* we both saw the same.'

Half afraid to, they compared memories. Everything tallied.

'I thought seals were coming through that door thing, at first,' said Ben.

'So did I, all tricky and clever like circus seals.' She breathed deeply. 'I don't understand any of it.'

'You know,' said Ben, 'I'm wondering about Mr Carrigan's coffee. I mean it *was* very strong, wasn't it? D'ye think anything was in it besides coffee?'

'Mr Carrigan would never do anything like that.' Aideen felt ashamed now of her own midnight suspicion.

'No, *he* wouldn't, but I'm not so sure about Lir Kinseely. He arranged everything else, didn't he? Including the boat, and the coffee too, I'll bet.'

'Could be.'

'Well, amazing things come into your head when you're drugged, and they seem as real as eating your breakfast. That stuff they gave me for my knee surgery did that. I'd forgotten until now.'

~

'Ah, sure,' Mr Carrigan said, an hour or so later (his hand was decidedly shaky as it vibrated Maddy's teacup back to its saucer) after explaining, as best he could, why the astronomy outing had changed so dramatically. 'Ah, sure, wasn't it all part of the bargain made between Lir and myself? Wasn't he to be meeting us at that very spot, and to bring the two new seals with him, the ones not able to find their way to the breeding places, for hasn't all that blasting and dynamiting closed up the right ways and opened up the wrong ones? If it wasn't for Lir knowing all the underwater passages like the palm of his hand, they'd be lost forever, poor creatures.'

The children exchanged a brilliant look.

'There'll not be a seal left alive soon enough, and if the ceiling is penetrated that'll be the end of it all.'

Again the children's glances held. All at once, Mr Carrigan and his brother's cross-purpose references to floor and ceiling, puzzling at the time, fell into place; whichever was which depended where your own world was, land or sea. There was only that shallow layer of water between them. If the fissure cracked further .... Mr Carrigan drew a sort of hiccuping breath and gestured towards Ben and Aideen. 'They understand the terrible damage of it all. Isn't that what we went to show them, Lir and myself, for they're the ones with the right feelings, same as yourselves, Mrs. Maddy, and sure we knew you wouldn't be minding at all once it was over and done.'

The sisters exchanged a wry smile and nodded gamely to comfort him as he expanded further, mystifyingly.

'He'll listen to children. He's a grand man, we know that. Doesn't he want Ox Island bird sanctuary left alone, and the foxes and wild flowers on it, too, and the whole coast line left free and natural ....' Mr Carrigan's gabbling was high speed.

'Er, er, *who*? Er, what?' asked Maddy, lost.

'Mr Wild Life that's who, and hasn't he just got himself voted onto the government so he can do it, that's what.'

'Er, what *is* what, Mr Carrigan?' asked Riona, still

baffled. '*Do* what?'

'Of course. The very man!' Maddy turned to her sister. 'He's a real individualist. Some people say he's eccentric and some say he's great, and I'm one of those. His one aim is to preserve every last scrap of wild life that's left around here, and to put a stop to the way those awful building developers are ruining the whole environment for future generations, like our grandchildren, if we ever have any. He's even had himself re-named John Wild Life instead of John Doyle, lawfully by Deed Poll, so people can't forget what he stands for. He certainly got my vote at election time.'

'There you are then.' Mr Carrigan was calmer. 'Lir and myself planned for the children to tell that to Mr Wild Life instead of us, maybe as if they'd found it out for themselves, exploring about a bit on their own. They wouldn't say *all* they'd seen, o' course.'

'Er, I'm still a trifle befogged,' Riona said, turning to the children. 'What *did* you see exactly?'

They hesitated until Mr Carrigan gave them the lead they needed.

'Just tell the things we showed you down there in the harbour,' he said, crisply, 'right from when we parked the van 'til you lay down for that bit of a "rest".' He leaned on the last word with a slight wink of one eyelid.

That's really spelling it out, Ben thought. Obediently, they retold each step, omitting Oisín-Below-the-Water but including Mr Kinseely's dramatic disappearance into the phosphorescent water layer at the bottom of the deep fissure. Their mothers' faces whitened.

'How was he supposed to get back up?' asked Maddy.

'And didn't you say the tide was on the turn?' said Riona. 'Wouldn't that ...?'

'It's like I told these two,' said Mr Carrigan, 'Lir knows every in-and-out of the seals' lanes and caverns down there, air holes and all; indeed doesn't he himself swim as good and better than any seal? And, anyway, wasn't it time for him to be back at his job?'

'Oh, back at his diving work?' Maddy remembered.

'Indeed yes, Mrs Maddy, his best work is done under the water.'

'It must take him away for long periods. I don't think I've ever met him all the time we've lived here,' said Maddy.

Mr Carrigan nodded. 'He can't abide being ashore, that's why. Many's the time he contacts me, though, to do a bit of work for him up here on dry land.'

'I see,' said Riona, 'like drawing public attention to the dangers threatening the seals' natural habitat.'

Mr Carrigan regarded her with delight. 'No one could say it better than that, not even that Mr Wild Life himself.' He swirled tea leaves around the bottom of his cup as intently as any fortune teller. 'Mrs Maddy, do you think the two of you ladies would work out how the children can meet that man? And Ben there, and Aideen and myself will be having a bit of a rehearse, so to speak, so they'll put it over real well.'

The children looked at one another, puzzled. They had obeyed Mr Carrigan's wink but it required further explanation.

He grinned at them. 'I haven't been to Flag o' the Woods since I was a chisler of a boy. How about the three of us going there now for a grand confabulation?'

~

'There'll be no fizzing here today,' Mr Carrigan said, sitting down on Flag o' the Woods' biggest tree stump with an easy air.

Ben's jaw dropped. 'How do *you* know about that?'

'Didn't I feel the same sort o' thing myself as a lad?'

'Mr Carrigan ....' Aideen wobbled inside but forced herself on. '... I think you ought to know what we, sort of — well — *dreamed* in the boat last night.' It was the politest way she could put it. 'Both of us saw, dreamed I mean, exactly the same. It was very, very strange ....'

'Like hallucinations,' Ben said.

'I've heard o' them,' smiled Mr Carrigan, 'a bit frightening, like nightmares, I've heard tell.'

'It didn't frighten us *as* we watched,' said Ben, 'because the people seemed to be so happy there, even ....' His eyes met Aideen's.

'Now where, and who, would you be meaning at all?' Mr Carrigan's warm blue eyes held theirs.

Aideen weighed each syllable. 'It was Oisín, well, almost Oisín.'

'Oisín-Below-the-Water is my name for it,' muttered Ben.

'Well, now, isn't that the grand name?' Mr Carrigan smiled.

'We saw Lir ...' Aideen began, slowly.

Ben rushed in impatiently, '*The Mac Alúishin fizz came from him.*' His stomach jerked as he said it.

'And Sea Foam, he was riding Sea Foam. *He* was the man we call the Mad Rider,' burst out Aideen.

'Doesn't that fella always expect a horse to be the same on land as in a storm at sea, divil mend him, frightening the daylights out o' ordinary folks like ourselves.' Annoyance flitted over Mr Carrigan's features. 'A bit more patience is what he needs instead o' wanting everything done the day before yesterday whenever he comes across a new seal in trouble. Hadn't I barely got the dotey creature mended and rested before he had to put him back in the water? And leaping Sea Foam off the cliff like that! No wonder someone noticed, and the helicopter was called out. Nearly got himself banjaxed that day, he did. Out o' his own element, o' course.'

Several twos and twos totted up in the children's heads during this waterfall of words, making sense, if they believed in the impossible, that is.

'It's too spooky,' said Ben. '*No one* can do such things, except ....' He stopped short.

'Not even in dreams? Or the hallucination things you said about?' Mr Carrigan's jutty eyebrows raised.

'Well,' Aideen began, 'the coffee ....'

'Your brother filled the flask, didn't he?' asked Ben, pointedly.

Mr Carrigan gave a throaty chuckle. 'Diver's coffee, he calls it. A kindly brew it is too.'

'So we *were* drugged,' Ben said.

A long pause hung in the air. 'Well, now, that's not a very nice thing you're saying, young feller-me-lad. Sure he only adds in a drop or two of the eye-opening mix the new seals need to get, but the effect wears off us folk in no time at all, and no harm done neither. Indeed I wish he'd let me have it a bit more often than he does. I do envy them down there many's the time.'

'Eye-opening mix? I ... see ...' said Aideen, doubtfully.

Mr Carrigan nodded. 'You did see, indeed you did. And there it'll stay inside your heads for always, whenever you need to believe it.'

'I do need to believe that Declan and Fintan can be up to their tricks just like they used to,' she admitted.

'Like Fintan firing off a catapult at the Isle of Man boat?' grinned Ben.

'Ah, now, that was a bit cheeky, but maybe I'd have done the same thing if that rudder blade cut me open,' said Mr Carrigan.

Which explains why Lir Kinseely went so wild when we said we were going to have a trip on it, thought Ben. 'But it *is* only a dream thing, isn't it?' he insisted, aloud.

'Seal people,' said Mr Carrigan, 'did you ever hear tell of the seal people?'

'Oh, yes,' Aideen replied, with confidence. 'I've read loads of folk tales and legends about them, and how they sometimes come ashore and take human form and' — her memory resurrected something else — 'and how some people can live on as seals ....'

'There you are then.' Dumbfounded, Ben watched Mr Carrigan's darkly flushed face as he continued. 'It's not *only* in the old days such things got told,' he said. 'Folk close to the sea know better. Taking human form, did you say? Would that be, maybe, after meeting a person they liked better than themselves on the land?'

'Well, ye — es,' said Aideen.

'They always end up having babies in those stories,' Ben snorted. He hated yucky stories like that.

'My own mother saw such a baby once,' announced Mr Carrigan.

Ben stared at him.

'A sea-child, she said it was, a beautiful baby, a boy. And she'd seen webs as thin as bat wings folding and unfolding between his fingers and toes.'

'Well, that was just a story.' Ben shifted uneasily.

'My mother was no liar, I'll tell you that.'

'Do shut up, Ben!' hissed Aideen. '*Listen*.'

Mr Carrigan smiled his forgiveness. 'Special people they grow up to be, she told me that too,' he went on, his voice soft and dreamy, 'but they must always work for the sea and what's in the sea. The older they get the stronger their powers and responsibilities, that's what she said.' He sighed deeply before falling into silence.

A thick mental fog swamped the children for some time.

'I'd like to know more about that baby,' Aideen said, at last. 'Would she tell us, do you think, Mr Carrigan?'

'Ah, God bless her, she left us long since,' said Mr Carrigan. 'Leaving me to watch over Lir. She knew his underwater ways would always be too wild and mischievous for the land ....'

'Like galloping Sea Foam all round the cliffs and Roshín Rock like a mad thing, and leaping him into the sea, d'ye mean?' said Ben.

'Isn't Sea Foam a horse of the sea?' said Mr Carrigan. 'The land's not for the likes of him at all, as I was telling Lir not long since.'

Ben's mind revolved. Underwater ways? A horse of the sea? What on earth ... well, that is not the right thing to say about all this he told himself, ruefully. He no longer felt sure what the right thing was, in any shape or form, except that Mr Carrigan's knack of sliding from real to unreal and back again somehow lightened the shadows in his mind.

Aideen's hesitant nodding betrayed her continued bewilderment. 'But the fizzing feeling we always get, Mr Carrigan. What about that?'

'Oh,' said he, 'didn't I tell you I felt it myself as a young chisler of a boyo, and some of my pals too, but they forgot when they grew up. Most folk do that, unless there's a reason for them to remember.' He paused. 'The two o' ye have a reason,' he said, then, 'the very same reason why ye will be doing that job for us with Mr Wild Life tomorrow.' He stood up, darting a quick glance towards the old oak tree on the Island before whisking himself off, his expression a little wistful. Their ears barely caught his self-absorbed murmuring. 'And that'll be enough for now, Lir Kinseely. No more queer birds, and all that. Get on with the work down there and give me a bit o' rest from your mischief and trickery for another while.'

Aideen shot Ben a deep, illuminated look. 'Kin,' she said, 'I've suddenly thought — aren't you and me kin to each other, you know, cousins?'

Now what? thought Ben.

'S.E.A.L.Y.' She spelled it out.

'Kin — seely. *Kinsealy!* Mr Carrigan's kin —' (Ben's memory clicked like a computer) '— that baby story his mother told him ... you can't mean ...?'

Aideen's voice was threadlike. 'Remember what Brains said: 'There are more things in heaven and earth, Horatio ....'

~

'I see,' said Brains, next morning, when he heard his favourite quotation end the amazing story told at Flag o' the Woods. He did not see but he was not going to admit it.

'There certainly is no fizz today,' said Nuala, her eyelids drooping.

'It's pretty rotten without it.' Micky frowned. 'I wish you'd told us, just the same, so we all could have seen your Mr Kinseely go down to, well, wherever it was he did go to.' Oisín-Below-the-Water lodged in his throat like a splinter.

'How could they, Micky O'Mara? Ben and Aideen promised not to, didn't they? *You* couldn't have kept that promise all day! I bet it was hard.'

'It was,' said Ben.

They heard Riona's shrill whistle.

'He's come.' Aideen leapt up. 'Come on, Ben. It's Mr Wild Life,' she told them. 'He's coming to see us. Mum contacted him last night. Wait, just wait!'

'We'll be right back and, this time we'll tell you every single thing, I promise,' grinned Ben.

And so they did.

~

Mr John Wild Life was a man after their own hearts. He listened, deeply. He believed, utterly. He acted, urgently. Within the week, his demands were met by the Powers That Be, seismic recordings registered, measurements taken, immediate restrictions placed upon any further explosive work in certain areas. Only he, Mr Carrigan and the children knew that this protected the 'ceiling' territory of Oisín-Below-the-Water, for so they continued to call it among themselves. As a result, the harbour's reconstitution was completed in time for the following summer, without a whit of harm to those below. The summer after that lawns and gardens took shape and blossomed; Mr Carrigan drove his bus around the Hill; Lir Kinseely reigned below and was never to be seen.

And so, summer after summer, in Whisky Cove, the friends from Flag o' the Woods swam and played in the sunshine. Seals often stationed themselves alongside the low wall of the Big Pool, sometimes erupting like corks from newly opened champagne bottles, briefly balancing on the tips of their tails in the water, one of them blatantly showing off his 'ladder' scar of stitching. And summer after summer, Mr Wild Life remained in touch with the children.

'Have you any further news?' he would ask them, wistfully.

'I've made a discovery!' gasped Aideen, after the latest such visitation. 'I know exactly why he's so eager to know all about Oisín-Below-the-Water.' She aimed an arrowlike glance deep into the eyes of each friend in turn. 'Next time he comes,' she breathed, softly, 'just you watch the way he spreads out his fingers when he's talking.'

'Webs,' said Brains, as if he had always known.